chew on and ponder which led me to deeper study of God's Word."

THE POWER OF GODLY INFLUENCE

"Great daily messages that give you reason to stop and think about how the verses can or should impact your life. Cathy Bryant is an amazing author and this one will not disappoint. Should be on everyone's nightstand for great thoughts to go to sleep with."

LIFE LESSONS FROM MY GARDEN

"I am loving every day that I read these devotionals. I appreciate being given the passages from the Bible to go along with the devotional. I also am glad to have the challenges to think deeply about the subject covered in relation to God's Word."

I0543884

What Readers Are Saying

TEXAS ROADS
"This is a heartfelt and sometimes heart-rending story; well-written, gripping, thoroughly enjoyable, and spellbinding."

A PATH LESS TRAVELED
"Cathy Bryant's delightful writing style will grab your attention and have you hoping the story never ends. You will find yourself laughing one minute and shedding silent tears the next."

THE WAY OF GRACE
"This may be the best book of this series so far – I absolutely could not put it down!"

PILGRIMAGE OF PROMISE
"I read many Christian books, but this one touched my heart more than any I have read."

A BRIDGE UNBROKEN
"I am new to this series but A Bridge Unbroken grabbed me, pulled me in, and kept me hostage until I had finished. Cathy Bryant is so very good at taking her readers and immersing them into the story in such a way that you are emotionally involved."

CROSSROADS
"Crossroads is one of those books that comes along and quickly finds its way into your heart."

STILL I WILL FOLLOW
"Cathy Bryant is now joining the ranks of my favorite authors. The Miller's Creek books are well written, realistic stories. She is not afraid to tackle tough issues and presents biblical responses to those issues that her readers can apply to their own lives. These books have blessed me and I encourage everyone to read them!

PIECES ON EARTH
"I enjoyed Pieces on Earth so very much, from both a fictional standpoint and also because of its spiritual themes. In this novella, Cathy has beautifully combined the power of story with one of the best presentations of the gospel message that I've ever seen."

THE FRAGRANCE OF CRUSHED VIOLETS
"I urge you, if you need to let go of something, no matter how big or small, take the time to read this book. Even if you think you are a forgiving person, like I thought I was, take the time to read this book. You won't regret it."

BELIEVE & KNOW
"Backed by Scripture and accompanied with thought provoking questions, this study will help you get grounded in the Word so you can talk to others about your own personal walk with God."

NEW BEGINNINGS
"When choosing a devotional to use during my daily Bible study, I look for one that has substance, or what Scripture refers to as meat. I can tell you that Cathy Bryant's New Beginnings fits the bill. Each one gave me something to

Evergreen

a Christmas Novella

CATHY BRYANT

WordVessel Press

Evergreen
© Cathy Bryant, 2019

WV **Published by WordVessel Press**
Texas

ISBN-13: 978-1-941699-21-8

To all my reader friends. You are such an inspiration and encouragement to me. Had it not been for you praying me through this book, I'm not sure it would exist. So thank you for reigniting my passion to write heart-stirring stories of God's unchanging grace. May He richly bless you and yours!

"But blessed is the man who trusts in the LORD, whose confidence is in Him. He is like a tree planted by water, that sends out its roots by the stream, and does not fear when heat comes, for its leaves remain green, and is not anxious in the year of drought, for it does not cease to bear fruit."
~Jeremiah 17:8

One

Ian's blood pressure shot through the roof as he eyed Ella's report card. What was going on with her anyway? She'd always been a straight-A student, but with each reporting period of the first semester of fourth grade, her grades had continued to fall, and this time there were two Fs. He looked up at his daughter who stood near the fridge with a blank look on her face. "Ella, do you want to explain what's going on with your grades?"

She gave a half shrug, as though she could care less.

He fought to control the anger that bubbled up inside. "I'll be calling the school to schedule a meeting with your teachers."

Ella still didn't respond, her face stony.

"And I'm sorry to have to do this, but you're grounded until you can bring these grades up."

Now her face contorted and turned purple with rage. "That's not fair! I can't help it if the teachers hate me."

Not the response he was looking for, but at least she was speaking now. "I'm sure they don't hate you, Ella."

"You never believe anything I have say." In a flurry of movement, she yanked her backpack off and slung it across the kitchen, catching the edge of a bowl and sending it crashing to the floor. Shards of the red bowl shattered across the room as Ella burst into tears."

Ian sidestepped the glass and took his daughter into his arms, stroking her hair. What was happening to them? Despair, dark and all-encompassing, shrouded his heart and mind as he searched for words that would help rather than send her into a fit of rage. "Feel like some dinner?"

She pulled away, wiping tears on her coat sleeves and shaking her head from side to side.

"You've got to eat something, sweetie." He thought back to this morning when he found most of yesterday's lunch still in her lunch box. "How about a burger and fries from Mel's?"

Without a word, she turned and left the room, the dragging shuffle of her footsteps sounding down the hallway.

Ian winced at the sound of Ella slamming the door to her room. Again. He smoothed down his beard, eyes to the ceiling. How long was this going to last? And could they ever return to what used to be?

He moved down the hall to Ella's room, gave a brief knock, and then opened the door. Once again, she was curled up in bed early, facing the wall. "Want me to read you a book, honey?"

"Dad, I'm ten."

As if he needed that reminder. "Okay, want to read me one?"

She flopped over and glared at him like he'd grown another head, or maybe horns. "Dad, stop trying to cheer me up."

He moved to her bed and sat down beside her. "This is the second night in a row that you've gotten mad and gone to bed early. Is everything okay?" He reached over and tucked a strand of hair behind her ear, searching her face for any clue into what was bothering her.

Ella stared back at him, her eyes dark and gloomy, her lips turned down at both corners. "Why don't you have any pictures of Mama anywhere in the house?"

His eyebrows shot up his forehead. How was he supposed to answer in a way that was both the truth and phrased so a ten-year-old could understand? "Well, I thought it would be easier on both of us not to have that reminder during the upcoming holidays."

She broke eye contact, sighed heavily, and once more turned her back on him. "I can tell it's going to be the worst Christmas ever."

"Oh c'mon, sweetheart, it won't be. We'll make it fun. Maybe Gigi and Poppy can come for a visit."

"Why can't we go see them?"

"Ella, you know it's peak season at the ski basin. I'll probably have to work both the day before and the day after Christmas."

"Great. Another thing to look forward to during the holidays." Only her voice held not a smidgen of excitement. "And just who's going to get stuck baby-sitting me during the time off from school?"

"Well, first off, I doubt seriously that anyone would call it 'getting stuck with you.' Second, I don't really know. Guess I haven't thought that far ahead."

A disgusted snort sounded from Ella's nose. "But yet you thought far enough ahead to take down all the pictures of Mama. Good night, Dad."

His heart lurched in his chest. Dad? What happened to her calling him Daddy? He leaned forward and kissed the back of her head, suddenly feeling weary. "Good night, Ella. Sleep tight. Don't let the--"

"Yeah, yeah, yeah."

A frown drew his eyebrows in tight as he dragged himself to a standing position. Over the past couple of years, ever since Amy's death, his daughter had changed drastically. No longer the carefree little girl he once knew, she'd turned sullen, moody, and often disrespectful. He'd hoped that time would make her better, but the opposite was happening. Instead she grew worse by the day. And no matter how hard he tried, nothing seemed to be working.

He rubbed at the tense muscles along the back of his neck and moved to the living room to stand near the rock fireplace, gazing into the flickering flames. His eyes unexpectedly filled with tears. "Dear God, help us." He whispered the words, careful not to draw Ella's attention. "I know it's been a long time since I talked to You, if I've ever talked to You. Guess I've been kind of mad about losing Amy." He stopped to wipe his eyes. "So I know I don't deserve to ask you anything, but I need Your help so badly. I'm at the end of my rope here, and I don't know what to do to help Ella. So please send someone to help us piece our lives back together. Someone who can bring my little girl back." There was no holding back the tears now. He leaned his head against the mantle and let them flow freely, even if they had to be silent tears for now.

"Please tell me you're joking." Holly's best friend, Darcy, raised her gaze to the high ceilings, shaking her head from side to side. "You've come up with some pretty scatterbrained ideas in the time I've known you, but this...well, this takes the prize for the worst ever."

Holly squelched the annoyance that built inside. It had taken a lot of courage to take this step, and in just a few words, Darcy had managed to bring back the worry that maybe this was a huge mistake. But she couldn't let Darcy in on that fear. "Oh, c'mon, quit exaggerating. It'll do me good. I happen to think it's a great idea." Holly leaned back against the counter in the kitchen of her New York City brownstone, took a sip of coffee, and forced her mind to consider the positives, like how much fun it would be to spend a white Christmas in the mountains, with the bluer-than-blue skies, rugged mountaintops, and the unmistakable smell of evergreens scenting the already-fresh air.

"Hello." Darcy stepped forward and waved a hand in front of Holly's face. "Earth to Holly. Come back to the conversation please." Her friend's eyes narrowed. "You're already there, aren't you?"

A broad smile stretched Holly's cheeks out, and a giggle escaped. "Yeah, I am."

"And where will you live? Huh? Have you thought about that?"

"Already taken care of. I'm going to be house-sitting."

"House-sitting for who? Someone you've actually met face to face?"

Holly shifted her weight and pretended to scratch a knee that didn't really itch. "Well, not exactly." She turned and headed to the living room, Darcy right on her heels. "But relax. I went through a reputable website."

"How many times have I tried to tell you that there are a bunch of mixed-up people out there? And in your profession, you should be plenty aware of that by now. What if this is some kind of ploy to get you to a mountain cabin in the boonies where..." A horrified expression covered Darcy's face.

Holly laughed and patted her friend's shoulder. "And that's why you're so good at writing fiction." She lowered her body down on the couch, careful not to slosh her coffee out the sides of her cup. "That's quite an imagination you have." But her friend's vivid word painting was already playing through the same scenario in her mind.

Darcy joined her on the couch. "And I suppose that Pollyanna positivity you have is why you're so good at yours."

Holly stared into her coffee cup. But was she truly good at her job? The same doubt she'd been feeling for weeks now enshrouded her inner being and knotted her eyebrows. How could she truly bring healing to others when she couldn't even heal herself? And the biggest question of all-- had she started her online business because the Lord willed it or because of her own attempts to mask her own pain?

Darcy's voice broke into her thoughts. "I'm really quite jealous. It must be nice to work from wherever you want."

"One of the perks of my job, for sure."

Her friend's shoulders suddenly slumped. "I can tell this is getting me nowhere."

"Please, Darcy. I need you to be happy for me. You know how I can get during the holidays. A change of scenery could be just the ticket for lifting my spirits."

"I do know how you can get, which is exactly why I want you here, where you'll be surrounded by people who love you."

Holly gave her head a definitive shake. "It's not fair to you and your family to always have me hanging around, spreading my gloom and sadness all over your Christmas holiday." Immediate gratitude flooded her heart for how they'd taken her in. She placed a hand atop Darcy's. "You know how much I appreciate all that you guys have done for me."

Her friend managed a half smile. "And we'll do it again, if you'll let us." A sudden thought brought a horrified look to Darcy's face. "You'll be all alone on Christmas Day."

"It won't be the first time." Holly took another sip of coffee. Yet another thought that often plagued her. Was she doomed to spend the rest of her life alone? She smiled at her friend. "Promise me that you won't be all worried and calling me every five minutes to see if I'm okay. Keep that overactive imagination for your stories, okay?"

"Easier said than done." Heavy sarcasm dripped from every word.

A laugh erupted from Holly's chest, instantly relaxing her muscles and lifting her spirits. "I see this trip as an opportunity to have a working vacation in a new location. It'll only be for a few months, and then--"

"A few months?" Alarm registered from every pore of Darcy's face. "I thought it would be just a couple of weeks!"

"Settle down. The people I'm house-sitting for are headed to Europe for a vacation, and I've agreed to take care of their place for them until they decide to return. I can't back out now."

Darcy threw a hand across her chest, over-dramatically gulping in air. "You're killing me here. No telling how many dangerous medical conditions you've unleashed in my body with your antics."

Another laugh burst forth. "Have I ever mentioned that I keep you around because you make me laugh?"

"Glad to be of service." Darcy frowned. "Hmmm, I don't think there are any positive reasons I keep you around."

Holly grabbed a pillow from the couch and slammed it into her friend's lap. "How about my positive attitude?"

"Well, there is that I suppose."

"And free therapy sessions during your bouts of writer's block."

"Okay, but let's not forget all the extra therapy I need with some of the stunts you pull--like this one."

Though Holly racked her brain for a comeback, nothing came. Instead, she once more let the siren's song of the Colorado Rockies lure her back into evergreen daydreams, oblivious to everything else.

"You're doing it again."

Holly sighed at the interrupted daydream. "Sorry."

Darcy glanced up at the big clock above the fireplace, and then jumped to her feet. "Is really already 8:30? I've got to go. And you have an appointment, right?"

"Oh!" Holly's mind raced through her giant to-do list. "And I've got some prep work to do first!" What was wrong with her?

She waved Darcy out the door, then sped to her office and started setting up for the screen time with one of her clients. Within a few minutes, she made the call, breathing deep to quell the tension that had built inside during the rush. "Hi, Jennifer!" Holly infused her voice with as much enthusiasm as she could muster. "How are you doing?"

"Okay, I guess." Defeat dogged Jen's expression. "I did really well with my exercise program early in the week, but when the weather turned colder, I just struggled to make myself get up and do it."

"Maybe that's the problem. We need to find ways for you to exercise so that you don't have to make yourself do it. Something you enjoy."

"Like what?"

"Was it the idea of going out in the cold that made you stay inside?"

Jennifer nodded. "Definitely."

"What are some things you could do instead of getting out in the cold? Things that you enjoy?"

Jennifer thought for a long minute. "You know, I really enjoy dancing."

"There you go. All you need to do is find an online program or maybe a DVD that you can use."

Her client's face brightened considerably. "I can do that."

"How was your sleep this week?"

"Good. At least earlier in the week." A visible light-bulb moment widened Jen's eyes. "That's when I slept better."

Holly nodded. "Yep. Remember what I said last week? Exercise improves sleep."

"That was definitely proved to me this week. When I exercised, I slept better. But when I didn't, my sleep suffered."

"And your diet?"

Evergreen

Light once more dawned on Jennifer's face. "Wow. I did great early in the week. I even lost a pound. But later in the week, I was so tired that I ate way too much comfort food and gained the pound back, plus some."

"It's definitely all connected. Are you making sure to get some sunlight every day or taking extra D3 when it's cloudy?"

The conversation continued for a few more minutes. By the time they ended the call, Holly had Jennifer pumped up and motivated for another week. Then it was on to more client calls, making contact with potential clients by phone or email, and writing an article for her blog. Finally, her work done for the moment, Holly pushed her chair back from the desk. How could she possibly take on so many new clients? But how could she possibly say no? These were people with real problems who needed her help. Plus she had to make a living somehow. Once more the questions concerning her work played chase in her head.

Holly wandered to the kitchen, made herself a cup of green tea, and curled up next to the fireplace. In spite of helping so many today, the familiar dark veil of depression descended on her and, tagging along behind, guilt. What a fake and phony she was. Why was it that she had helped so many with their depression, but still struggled with her own?

Oh, Lord, help me get better. Help me find out what I need to do to leave the past behind and move forward with my life.

Would the trip to Colorado truly help, or was it just a form of escapism? Her thoughts returned to the earlier conversation with Darcy. How would she cope with the holiday blues without her support system nearby? She literally knew no one in Colorado.

Determined to shake off the darkness and find answers, Holly rose to her feet. She might not have the answers now, but she knew the One who did. She had talked to Him in prayer. Now it was time to let Him talk to her through His Word.

Holly moved to a nearby accent table and picked up the Bible with a well-worn cover. She ran a hand over the old leather Bible imprinted with Mama's name, once more fighting back against a flood of memories, both happy and sad. She swallowed against the knot in her throat, returned to the sofa, and flipped open the pages, landing in the book of Jeremiah. Within a few minutes of reading, she found a verse that resonated in her soul. She reached for her pen, underlining the words that had latched hooks into her heart.

"But blessed is the man who trusts in the LORD, whose confidence is in Him. He is like a tree planted by water, that sends out its roots by the stream, and does not fear when heat comes, for its leaves remain green, and is not anxious in the year of drought, for it does not cease to bear fruit."

Hey, hadn't she read something similar yesterday in Psalms? She quickly leafed back to the first chapter of that book. Yes, there it was.

*"How blessed is the man who does not walk in
the counsel of the wicked, nor stand in the path of sinners,
nor sit in the seat of scoffers! But his delight is in the law of
the Lord, and in His law he meditates day and night. He
will be like a tree firmly planted by streams of water, which
yields its fruit in its season and its leaf does not wither;
and in whatever he does, he prospers. The wicked are not
so, but they are like chaff which the wind drives away.
Therefore the wicked will not stand in the judgment,
nor sinners in the assembly of the righteous. For
the Lord knows the way of the righteous, but the way of the
wicked will perish."*

She read both passages over and over again out loud,
then leaning her head back against the sofa, let the words
seep down deep. How easy it was to inadvertently adopt
the world's ways without a conscious decision to do so. So
easy to step away from the Lord. Is that what had happened
after the accident? Had she been so focused on healing
herself that she jumped into her current line of work
without waiting on God? Well, the key to not letting that
happen was to stay near to the Lord through meditating on
His Word and applying it to her life. That was her spiritual
sustenance.

A sudden connection drew her eyes back to her Bible,
one of those moments where she knew God's Spirit was
leading her. Yes, she was blessed, but it wasn't enough to
just live in that blessing. Instead, she was meant to bless

others by flourishing and fruiting. The thought brought comfort.

But the question still remained. Had she tried to flourish and be fruitful in her own strength, even adopting worldly wisdom, without fully leaning on God for it to happen? For surely there could be no true success that way.

Her eyes moved back to the verses and landed on the word "chaff." Refuse, trash, once close to the life-giving kernel of wheat, but eventually whisked away in whichever way the wind blew. Those were the people she needed to be reaching out to, not just with ways to improve their physical health, but in order to lead them to the Lord.

Immediate fear descended. Wouldn't many then reject her help because it stepped over into a realm they didn't want to consider?

Her heart burst into spontaneous prayer. "Lord, I want to be like that tree, so help me to keep my trust in You, no matter the circumstances or whatever happens as a result." Her mind replayed, with vivid accuracy, the string of disastrous events that often plagued her steps, especially during the Christmas season. "I want my roots to be planted deep in You, because You are living water. Help me not to hoard Your blessings, but to share them. And keep me from fear, which comes straight from the enemy." Oh, the fear, the debilitating fear that would take over if she allowed it even the smallest space.

What was the word that the verse in Jeremiah used? Drought. Yes, it was a drought in every sense of the word. Life-stealing. "Oh God, sometimes it feels like this drought will last forever." A half-sigh, half-sob tumbled from her lips, as she once again faced the overwhelming pain in her heart. "Help me let go of that anxiety, trusting that Your grace, that life-giving river where You've transplanted me, is more than enough, no matter how this all plays out." She swiped at tears that had somehow leaked from her eyes without permission. "Keep me ever green and bearing fruit for You as I move past what's behind and press forward to what You have for me down the road. In the precious name of Jesus I pray."

But what in the world did a working holiday vacation in Colorado have to do with any of it?

Two

The next morning Holly had to drag herself out of bed. The night had been one of tossing and turning, as she wrestled with her conflicted thoughts.

What had happened? Yesterday she'd been so excited about the prospect of house-sitting in a small mountain town. Now she was questioning her sanity.

She stumbled into her slippers, donned her warm robe, and groggily made her way to the kitchen for a cup of coffee.

Though the coffee helped wake her up a bit, it did nothing to relieve the conflict within. On one hand, she just could not suffer through another Christmas in New York City. Nor was it fair to Darcy and her family to have to put up with her. But on the other hand, maybe Darcy was right about some things. It would be a huge challenge without her support system nearby, especially this time of the year. And what if this cabin was in the boonies like Darcy suggested? Holly shuddered. Maybe she should pursue a different line of thought.

She headed back to her bedroom, put on her workout clothes, along with a warm jacket, ear band, and mittens, and headed out the door of her apartment for a jog.

Stepping out into the cold morning air was another jolt to her grogginess, and within a couple of blocks she felt the endorphins starting to kick in and pep her up to her usual self.

An hour and a half later, she sat, cleaned and dressed, behind her computer and dialed her client in London. When Eleanor's face popped onto the screen, Holly smiled broadly. "Hi, El! How are you?"

"Believe it or not, it's been a surprisingly great week."

"That's good news."

"But I'm glad you called, because I do have a question."

Holly nodded. "Let's hear it."

"A colleague of mine invited me to spend Christmas with her and her family at a lovely country cottage. I said yes, but now I'm questioning if it was smart to respond so quickly."

"Why are you questioning it?"

"Well, this is a hard time of the year for me."

As it was for herself and so many others. "I understand that."

"I don't want to be a downer for them. No one wants a blooming gloomy Eeyore for a Christmas guest."

"Then don't be that person."

"I was talking to another friend about it, and he said he thought it was a terrible idea. Do you think I should back out?"

This conversation couldn't be just a coincidence. Was this the Lord's way of answering her prayer for His guidance in her own dilemma? "What do you want to do?"

"I want to do something different this year. I think perhaps a change of pace would be really good for me, you know?"

"Then that's what you should do. You should never listen to your fears or your naysayers." Good advice for Eleanor and herself.

"I love that! Hold on, let me jot that down." Eleanor grabbed a pen and paper and started writing away. "Never listen to your fears or your naysayers. Oh my goodness, but that's exactly what I was doing. I was fearful of what might happen, and then I was listening to others tell me it was a bad idea. Thank you, Holly."

"Glad to have helped." The rest of the conversation was all about the same types of things they always talked about: nutrition, exercise, sleeping patterns and more. And the two ended their conversation at the exact half hour mark.

Holly leaned over and looked at her schedule. No more appointments until this afternoon.

She stood, a grin on her face. If the trip to Colorado was in her future, some things needed to be purchased beforehand. No more listening to her fears or her naysayers.

Three hours later, she returned to her apartment, packages in tow. She'd found a couple of sweaters that, while not exactly Christmas-y, still had that Colorado-mountain-ski-lodge feel to them. In addition, she'd found matching leggings and the cutest leather snow boots she'd ever seen, with a band of fluffy brown fur around the top.

Just for fun, she put on one of the sweaters, a pair of leggings, and her new boots. Perfect! Excitement mounted. Yes, this was the right call to make. Though it might not always be easy--it was still life after all--this was exactly what she needed. And the best part was knowing that the Lord was with her.

She hurried to the kitchen and fixed a salad for lunch, then moved to her computer to research tourist attractions near the town where she'd be house-sitting. Popping a bite of salad in her mouth, she clicked her cursor on the search window and typed in the town's name. Only as she saw the words "Evergreen, Colorado" in the search bar did she do a double take. Evergreen. Just like the verse from Jeremiah that she'd read last night. She reached for her Bible to read it again, flipping a few pages. Ah, here it was.

"But blessed is the man who trusts in the LORD, whose confidence is in Him. He is like a tree planted by water, that sends out its roots by the stream, and does not fear when heat comes, for its leaves remain green, and is not anxious in the year of drought, for it does not cease to bear fruit."

Its leaves remain green, and it wasn't anxious in the year of drought. How like the Lord to keep bringing her back to the same verse, so she could meditate on it and draw sustenance, just like those tree roots in the verse.

Evergreen. It was so difficult to keep living in the shadow of death and rejection. Only as she leaned on God was she somehow able to make it through, and this trip would be no different.

Fresh excitement for the adventure that lay ahead of her coursed through her veins. She turned back to her computer. In a short amount of time, she'd made her travel arrangements and a bucket list of all she wanted to do and enjoy during her trip. At the top of her list was one item that both excited and scared her. Snow skiing. And she'd just made online reservations for lessons.

A sinking feeling inside brought on yet another question. Had she lost her ever-loving mind?

Three days later, Holly's mouth gaped open as she drove her rental Jeep down the mountain with the town of Evergreen spread out in the valley below. Stunning! Just like a postcard. The sunshine sparkled off a lake, making the whole thing feel surreal. She cracked open a window and breathed deep from the fresh mountain air. Even better than she'd expected.

A happy sigh sounded. So this was what love at first sight felt like.

As she neared the bottom of the hill that led into town, she pushed the GPS button. She'd programmed in the address of her house-sitting gig earlier that day and followed the directions of the overly-pleasant voice.

Her jaw once more unhinged at all the beautiful lodge-like cabins in the area. But she slowed the SUV to a crawl at a smaller, less conspicuous cabin nestled between several tall evergreens and a small stream. "It looks just like a scene in a snow globe." Her voice held joyous awe. So homey and cozy, and so unlike the big city. Just what she needed.

The next driveway past that property was her house-sitting gig. This cabin was definitely on the lodge-like scale rather than the homey smaller cabin she'd just passed. But it would do, even if she'd be the only one staying in it. At least it wasn't the cabin-in-the-boonies scenario that Darcy had painted. From outward appearances, it looked as though the place could house at least three families. Just the thought of the word 'family' sent her heart into a temporary tailspin, but she quelled it with a few deep breaths. She exited the vehicle, pulled out her luggage, and moved to the front door, a massive, hand-carved job that reeked of rustic charm.

She punched in the code Annie Davis had given her over the phone, and the door opened like a charm. After a tour of the house, she quickly gobbled down a peanut butter sandwich, then headed back out to the Jeep. Yes, she was running a bit behind schedule for her first ski lesson, but she should be able to easily make up the deficit on her trip up to the ski resort.

A happy hum broke loose from her heart and her throat. This was shaping up to be the best Christmas she'd had in a very long time.

Ian pulled his Subaru into Dave and Miranda's driveway, grabbed the box of requested ornaments, and carried them inside.

Miranda stood at the stove stirring something that smelled like Christmas fudge, while Dave stood nearby, obviously enjoying conversation with his wife. They both turned to look at him as he entered.

"Hey, guys." He tiptoed over to his cousin and gave her the customary peck on the cheek. "How's my favorite cousin?"

She smiled back at him. "Good, but I think you mean only cousin."

"Okay, my favorite only cousin." He turned to give Dave a man hug, complete with two obligatory back slaps.

"Ella with you?" Miranda continued to stir as she asked the question.

"Nope, it's your day to pick her up, remember? I was just on my way to work and decided to drop off the box of Grandma's ornaments that you requested." He sat them down on the counter.

She wiped her hand on a towel. "Are you sure you don't need them?"

"Absolutely not. They've just been sitting in the attic gathering dust."

"You could've used them to celebrate Christmas, you know. Decorating a tree might help Ella get back to her normal self."

So she'd noticed it too. Definitely something to discuss with her sometime, but not today. Time to change the subject. "What do you all have going on this weekend? Maybe we could have dinner together."

"I was just about to invite you over here for Saturday night. We're having some people over." A mischievous glimmer flickered in her eyes.

Uh oh. "What's her name?"

"Delia, and she's really nice."

"While I appreciate your ongoing quest to fix me up, I just remembered that we have other plans."

Dave chuckled. "Told you it wouldn't work."

She frowned at both of them. "I just thought maybe you were ready to get back in the game."

He gave his head a vehement shake. "I don't want to get back in the game. It's too difficult. So I've decided to change the rules and not play the game at all."

Miranda made a face. "Ha! Very funny. But honestly, Ella needs a mother, Ian. Surely you realize that."

"No, she needs to recover first." And at this rate, would that ever happen? "And I'm not ready either. So please stop."

He turned and strode from the house with Miranda's disappointed eyes staring after him, but it couldn't be helped. She had to learn that her ploys to get him hitched were useless. The last thing he needed was to rush into a relationship to try to ease the heartbreak that both he and Ella felt.

Just as he started the vehicle, his phone rang. "Hello?"

"Ian? Oh my goodness, I'm so glad I caught you."

"Annie? Is that you?"

"Yes. John and I are in Europe. I was going to call you before we left and totally forgot. Can you do me a favor?"

"Sure." Just what he needed right now. Someone else who wanted a piece of him, at a time of the year where he didn't have many pieces left. And to top it all off, they were coming up on the anniversary of Amy's death, when Ella needed him more than ever.

"We have a house-sitter coming in either today or tomorrow to watch over things while we're away. Could you look in on her when you have a few minutes?"

"Uh, her?" Was this some convoluted way that yet another female was trying to run his personal life?

"Yes, dear. She sounded very nice on the phone."

Very nice? As compared to what? A barracuda? "Uh, I'll see what I can do. I was just on my way to work." And a full slate of afternoon lessons.

"I'm sure tomorrow will be fine. Thank you so much. You and Ella have a marvelous Christmas."

"You too." He hung up, shoulders sagging. Yeah, a marvelous Christmas wasn't gonna happen for them. And their not-so-marvelous Christmas was already off to a less-than wonderful start.

Three

Holly bounded from her rented Jeep with a fresh spring in her step. As she strode across the parking lot toward the main lodge, she peered up at the bright blue skies tickled by the tops of velvety green pine boughs. She breathed in deeply.

If only someone could figure out how to bottle all this--especially the smell. Now that would make a great business endeavor.

She climbed stairs, wet with soggy, melting snow, and hurried inside to the counter. Yes, she was running a wee bit behind, but it shouldn't be any big deal, right?

The woman behind the counter smiled broadly. "Welcome to Evergreen Ski Resort. How may I help you?"

"Hi. My name is Holly Richfield, and I have a reservation for a ski lesson. Since this is my first time to ski, I don't have a clue about what I'm supposed to do."

The woman's smile had completely disappeared, replaced by an aggravated flat line to her lips. "I'm sorry, but our last lessons for the day started an hour ago."

"But I already paid for the lesson online. I would've been here sooner, but I got behind this huge snow plow on my way up the mountain, and there was no getting around it. Now can I please have my lesson?" The woman huffed out a sigh, turned to her computer, and started typing furiously. "Tell me your name again."

"Holly Richfield." At just that moment, the door behind her swung open, letting in a wintry breeze. Holly turned to look.

Silhouetted against the bright sunlit windows was a really tall and broad-shouldered guy, his funky-looking boots clicking against the floor as he made his way to the counter. He came and stood beside her. With a nod of his head in greeting, he turned toward the girl behind the counter. "Hey, Nicole. I'm headed home for the day. Do you mind signing me out?"

Nicole briefly replaced her tight lips with a smile reserved only for him and replied, "Um, your two-thirty lesson just showed up."

Holly stuck out a hand. "Hi. I'm Holly." She infused her voice with confidence and enthusiasm and smiled as big as she could. "I was just telling Nicole that I'm running a bit behind because I was behind a gigantic snow plow on the way up the hill. And that road--so twisty and windy and narrow--there was absolutely no way for me to pass."

His eyes narrowed, and he nodded, but said nothing.

Holly turned her attention back to Nicole. "So, if you will just tell me what equipment I need and where I pick that up, I'm sure that Mr....?" She looked over at the guy whose bulky clothing reminded her of a cross between the Jolly Green Giant, the Michelin Man, and the Pillsbury

Dough Boy, hoping he'd fill in the blank she'd left hanging in mid-air.

But again he said nothing. This time a little hint of--was it contempt?--lay in the depths of the man's really blue eyes.

She again faced Nicole. Well, if he wasn't going to be polite enough to at least give her his name, she'd just invent one instead. "...Mr. Jolly Michelin Dough Boy would be happy to give me the lesson I've already paid for online." She faced him once more, replacing her quickly-growing irritation with a pasted-on smile. "And I'll be sure to give him a really nice tip since I was late, even though it was truly beyond my control." She ignored the sneer that landed on Dough Boy's face, and turned her attention back to Nicole.

Nicole exchanged a knowing glance with the man and then opened her mouth to speak.

But the man beat her to it. "It's okay, Nicole. I've got this."

"Thank you."

He was already walking away, but called back over his shoulder. "If you'll follow me, Polly, I'll make sure that we get you everything you need for that lesson."

"It's Holly." She quickly grabbed her things and half-ran to catch up to him. "In a few seconds' time they stood in a darker and more-crowded area of the building where several guys behind the counter were taking other customer's equipment, cleaning it, and putting it away.

"Hey, Jerry. We have a latecomer, but I'm going to go ahead and give her a lesson. She looks pretty athletic. Let's get her the narrow skis."

Jerry's eyebrows arched quickly, but he did as he was told. "As he laid her skis on the counter, he pointed to deeper into the crowded room. The ski boots are down there."

But Mr. No-Name looked at her directly. "I'm guessing you brought ski bibs, a ski coat, and some ski socks?"

She shook her head from side to side. Who knew you needed special clothes?

"Then we need to go to the ski store before we fight the crowd to rent your boots."

A few minutes and a couple of hundred bucks later, Holly exited the store with her gear and her skis in tow. Now she struggled to follow Mr. Not-So-Jolly down the narrow and crowded corridor to rent her boots. Without meaning to, she whacked at least two people with her skis. Wow, this looked so much easier in the movies.

After renting her boots, she added them to the pile of stuff she carried. Would it hurt her ski instructor to at least offer to help?

He turned and faced her. "The changing rooms are at the back. I'll wait out front at the counter."

"Um, okay. Uh, can you tell me how to get back there? This place is like a maze."

He pointed to the bright spot at the other end of the crowded space. "Head toward the light and you should find it." With that he clomped away in his ski boots with great strides, quickly disappearing in the swarm of people.

A half hour later, doing her best to walk through the space with boots she couldn't get completely fastened and skis that she'd only figured out how to put on because a nice lady changing clothes explained how they worked. As she walked, half-slid, down the area, hollering out "Excuse me!" so she'd be heard by those in front of her, she couldn't help but notice that people were staring at her, then nudging their friends, pointing, and laughing behind their hands.

"Well, it doesn't help that these skis keep crossing each other," she said to herself as she finally made it back to the front room.

True to his word, Mr. Whoever leaned against the counter, chatting with Nicole. When he saw her, he laughed out loud. Not a soft chuckle, but a knee-slapping guffaw. To his credit, he quickly brought his laughter under control, regained his stony-faced expression, and stepped over to her. "Uh, Molly...it usually works best if you don't put your skis on until you get to the actual snow."

"It's Holly, like the bush, and how was I supposed to know that? This is my first time to ski."

A slow, Grinch-like grin spread across his face. "I wish I could fully express just how much I'm looking forward to your lesson." He turned and headed to the door, not giving her time to take the skis off.

She turned toward Nicole one last time to wave goodbye, then headed after him. When she finally caught up, completely out of breath and her heart pounding furiously, she gave him the biggest smile she could muster. "So. Are you and Nicole a couple?"

"Not exactly, though I think she would like that."

Holly rolled her eyes. Typical macho man thought. "Well, she definitely has good taste."

"Thank you."

"I was referring to her sweater." She tried to keep the catty grin off her face when he looked her way, but there was no controlling it.

He stopped in his tracks, but she kept ski-walking toward the lesson area which lay directly ahead. Hopefully she'd taught him that she could both take it and dish it out. She reached her destination and somehow managed to turn around as he came toward her.

Uh oh. Based on the expression on his face, it was not going to be a pleasant afternoon.

Holly breathed deeply, though for some reason, even the outdoors seemed extremely short on oxygen. She squared her shoulders, and gave herself an inside-her-head pep talk. This will be fun. Learning new things is good for you. Meeting new people can be a positive experience. Think about all the exercise you'll be getting in such beautiful surroundings.

Coach Dough Boy was beside her now, his lips completely flat, his voice level at monotone autopilot setting. "We're going to start by learning a few positions with your skis." On his little short wide skis he turned his knees inward so that his ski tips touched each other in front. "This is called the snow plow position, and we use it to slow our speed or to stop. You try it."

She moved in front of him and tried to position her skis in the same way. But his easy-looking move wasn't as easy as it appeared. Her skis kept crossing and then without warning she started going backwards down the hill. "Help! What do I do?"

He hollered out something, but about that same time a ginormous machine on the next hill over started making noise and blowing snow.

"What? I can't hear you!" And she was picking up speed.

This time he demonstrated what he wanted her to do by picking up one ski and turning it sideways to an outward-facing position.

"I can't do that!"

He raised both hands and shoulders in a shrug, then started toward her on his skis.

But before he got anywhere close, Holly decided to give the demonstrated maneuver a try. But as she turned the raised ski outward, it dipped and caught in the snow. In a flash, she was flying through the air out of control. When she finally came to a stop, she was flat on her back, eyes squeezed shut. She laid there for a second, afraid to move. Had she broken any bones?

When she opened her eyes and looked up, her ski instructor--what was his name anyway?--stood over her. "You okay?"

There was no way she could rein in her fury. "What kind of teacher are you? I could've died or been seriously hurt."

"Trust me, lady. If you can still talk, there's nothing wrong with you."

"But I'm on this huge hill, and I've never even skied before."

He pulled her to her feet and then went to retrieve her skis which had fallen off somewhere along the way. In no time at all he was back at her side. "Let's get one thing straight. This is not a big hill." He pointed behind her. "That's a big hill."

She turned at the waist and looked behind her. Her mouth fell open. What appeared to be a giant white cliff rose out of the ground so high, she had to crane her neck back to see the top. Surely that wasn't the next step of her ski lesson. She turned back to face him. "What did I do wrong? I really want to do better."

Something about his face seemed to soften immediately. "Let me go exchange these skis for something a little easier. You stay here."

He was only gone for about five minutes, and the new skis he brought back worked like a charm. The snow plow maneuver was now much easier, and this time he had her turn to face downhill instead of allowing her to do it her way. Within a few short minutes, she had made it down the small slope that--as he'd correctly pointed out--bore no resemblance to the monster beside them.

She turned, triumphant. "I did it! Now how do I get back up so I can do it again?"

In a flash, he swooshed in on his skis and demonstrated how to sidestep up the mountain.

Within only a few steps, she was huffing and puffing. "I thought there were some kind of mechanized lifts."

"There are, but not for small hills like this."

Yeah well, try telling that to her thighs, which burned as if she'd just finished running a marathon. And the lack of air! By the time she reached the top, her heart was pounding, she could only gulp in air through her mouth, and her lungs felt like shriveled balloons. Then, as if she needed anything else, her surroundings began to spin. Since she couldn't speak, all she could do was plop down on her knees in the snow, her skis popping off behind her. She leaned over, hoping it might help, but all it did was encourage the regurgitation process. After she finished throwing up the remains of her peanut butter sandwich, he came over to pick up her skis and help move her away from what was left of her lunch.

"If you don't mind me asking, how long have you been in the mountains?"

Still feeling sickly, she managed to squeak out, "Just got here today."

His eyes widened. "Don't you know that you need to give your body time to adjust to the altitude before physical exertion?"

"Didn't know." The words barely wheezed out, her lungs still pleading for oxygen.

"How long since you've had something to drink?"

"Not since lunch."

He shook his head in exasperation. "I'll be back in a second. Have a seat on that bench." He handed her skis to her and quickly skied off toward the lodge, making it look so incredibly easy. She huffed out a disgusted sigh. Dough Boy was also a big show-off.

A minute or two later he returned with a cup of water and handed it to her. "You really need to stay hydrated up here. It's a very dry climate, and when you get dehydrated it makes altitude sickness even worse."

There was actually a thing called altitude sickness? She sipped the water slowly, fearful that it would just come right back up. Thankfully, it did not. Instead her head began to clear, and it got easier to breathe. "Mr....what's your name again?"

"Ian. Ian Duffee."

"Ian, are we done for the day?"

"You still have some time coming if you feel up to it."

Holly nodded. She stood and snapped on her skis, which took several tries. "I think I can make it if I take things slowly."

"Are you sure?" The look that accompanied his question told her that he thought she was already moving at paint-drying speed, but to his credit, he only nodded. "Let me show you the best way to fall before we go down again."

Well, if there was a best way to fall, why didn't he show it to her before she almost broke her neck?

"If you can't slow down or want to control your fall, lean your knees toward one direction and kind of sit down sideways. Try it."

She accomplished the task on the first try. Well, at least she was good at falling.

"Do you have any idea of how to get up?"

She looked at her skis. Putting them either in front or in back and actually being able to stand up was out of the question, as proved by her lunch-losing process. The skis had popped off as soon as her knees hit the ground. Holly raised her head his way, grimaced, and shook her head from side to side.

He demonstrated the procedure, which was basically just falling in reverse.

But no matter how hard she tried, she was just too weak and winded to make it happen.

Finally he stepped in and came to her rescue. "Here. Let me help you up this time. You can practice this at home without skis until it gets easier."

Well, of course it would be easier without skis, but how would that help if--and that was a mighty big if at this point--she ever decided to risk her life again. But as she skied down the slope again, a thrill of exhilaration built inside her. So much so that she forgot to take into consideration that she was gathering speed.

Ian called out behind her. "Snow plow! You're almost to the fence!"

But she panicked, and to make things worse, her skis refused to cooperate. She once more landed in a heap just a few inches in front of the fence. The combination of her fatigue from the long trip coupled with her humiliation caused unexpected and uncustomary tears to unleash.

Ian reached her side in a few seconds time to find her in full ugly-cry mode. His face and eyes took on immediate concern. "Hey, it's okay. Don't cry."

"I'm sorry," she wailed, her chin trembling. "It's just been a really long and hard day."

He helped her to her feet. "Let's go sit on the bench. He held her arm and coached her over to where they both took a seat.

Ian lowered his head for a second before raising it again and looking her full in the face. "I owe you an apology, Holly. I was a little put out because you showed up expecting a lesson when I could have been picking up my little girl from school. But I shouldn't have treated you the way I did."

It wasn't often that she met guys who were willing to admit when they messed up. "Thank you." Now it was time for her to follow suit. "I had no idea how involved all this was, or that was there such a thing as altitude sickness."

A gentle chuckle parted his lips into a smile. "Well, now you know."

"I'm really sorry I kept you from picking up your little girl. Did your wife have to take off from work to go get her?"

His smile faded. "No. My--uh, wife died the year before last. My cousin picked her up." He hesitated a minute. "I just like to pick her up when I can because Ella's gone through a rough time ever since her Mama died."

Holly's heart felt like it might burst out of her chest. "I'm so sorry. But actually, I might be able to offer some help. I operate an online health and wellness business where I help people with all kinds of issues, including grief management. If there's anything--"

He held up a gloved hand. "No, really, I appreciate the offer, but we'll get it figured out." The look on his face told her that he didn't want to hear anymore about it.

Now the air once more felt uncomfortable, but for a different reason. Time to give them both a break for the day. "I think I'm done for today, and I know you need to get home." She offered him a handshake, which he accepted. "Thank you for the lesson, Ian. I'll be in Evergreen for a while, so I might be contacting you again-- after I've adjusted to the lack of oxygen here--and schedule another lesson."

"Sounds good. You really did very well under the circumstances."

Holly laughed. "Which circumstances? The part where I threw up, or the part where you tried to kill me?"

His laughter joined her own as he helped her stand, grabbed her skis, and threw them over his shoulder. Then he helped her back to the lodge to turn in her rented equipment.

Before she left for the day, she handed him one of her business cards.

He eyed it skeptically.

"No pressure, Ian, but if there's ever anything I can do to help, please give me a call." She would have loved to explain that she had a degree and special training and plenty of success stories from her clients, but he obvious wasn't ready to hear it. Instead she just sent a smile. "Thanks again."

His return smile was genuine. "Thanks, Holly."

Only two thoughts played in her brain as she made her way to the Jeep.

At least she was still alive, and at least he finally got her name right.

But as she made her way down the mountain, her thoughts turned in a completely different direction. Perhaps the Lord had brought her to Evergreen, not just so she could hopefully avoid the Christmas blues, but so she could offer help and hope to a grieving widower and his hurting little girl.

The last thing Holly wanted to do when she got home was get ready for an evening appointment, but she didn't really have much choice. After a quick hot shower, she donned warm fuzzy pajama bottoms with a more professional shirt and set about getting everything set up.

About fifteen minutes before the screen chat, she turned on her computer and set about the process of hooking up to the internet. But for some reason, every time she tried to connect, she got nothing.

As the clock hands inched ever closer to time for her appointment, panic began to set in. In a flurry, she raced downstairs to find the note Annie had left her. She picked up the sheet of paper and scanned it quickly. Ah, there it was. The phone number of someone who could help. She quickly punched in the number. Finally, after the fourth ring, a voice answered.

"Hello?"

"Yes, I'm house-sitting for Annie and John, and they gave me your number if I needed help with anything. I'm having trouble getting the internet going."

He hem-hawed a moment, then finally go to the point. "Look, I'm not sure there's anything I can do. A lot of folks around here are still without internet because of a big forest fire this past summer."

Her eyes narrowed. Yeah, right. This guy just didn't want to help. "What in the world does a forest fire have to do with internet service?"

His voice took on a tinge of annoyed anger. "The fire damaged a lot of lines. It has taken them a while to get everything repaired, including some in town."

Holly looked out the window. Nothing but snow. And absolutely no evidence of a fire. "I don't see any burned trees out my window."

A heavy sigh sounded through the phone, as though the man was trying to control his ire. "We'll be right over to check it for you, ma'am." Then the line went dead.

In a couple of minutes the doorbell rang, and Holly rushed to open it. But when she saw who stood on the other side, she was tempted, at least momentarily, to close it again. Dough Boy. Had he not had a sad-faced little girl standing right beside him, she probably would have slammed it quickly--especially considering the angry expression on his face at the moment.

A curt laugh sounded from his mouth. "I should've guessed when you wouldn't take no for an answer." He strode past her and into the house, the little girl right behind him. "Where's the modem?"

Holly pointed to a counter in the kitchen. "Right there."

"And you've typed in the code?"

"Yes."

He made his way to the modem, took one look, and turned to face her. "It's not working. Just like I said. There's no internet."

Her eyes widened in more panic. "But I have an online appointment with a client like right now."

Ian scanned her clothing choice, one eyebrow cocked upward. "Not on your computer you don't. Can't you do it on your phone?"

Her face felt like it was turning fifty shades of purple as she inwardly berated herself. Her phone! Why hadn't she thought of that? She eyed the kitchen clock as she shooed them from the house and shut the door, making a mental note to apologize profusely the next time she saw them. Then with her heart pounding at ninety to nothing, she took the stairs two at a time to get to her files for a phone number.

Four

Fifteen minutes early. Perfect! Just enough time to put on her ski stuff and head out to the slopes.

Holly turned off the Jeep, gathered her gear, and stepped across the parking lot to the lodge. It had taken more than a little courage to get back on this particular horse after her less-than-stellar first lesson. But she'd forced herself to come back every day of her first week in Evergreen. Maybe today she'd be ready for a bigger slope and even learn to maneuver the ski lift.

True to form, Ian waited for her in the ski lesson area. He looked up as she neared, and that charming boyish grin of his softened his chiseled features. "Hey, Holly."

"Hey, yourself. How's it going?" She watched his face carefully, her radar honed in to pick up even the smallest clue.

His lips clamped together, his shoulders slumped, and a soft sigh sounded from his nostrils. "Just okay, but if it's okay with you, I'd rather not talk about it right now."

She nodded. "Fair enough. But you can't keep stuffing it down, Ian. At some point you're going to have to deal with it, or it will deal with you."

He nodded, but his face also darkened. "Yeah, I know. And if it's okay, I'd like to treat you to coffee after our lesson. That is, if you have time to talk."

"I'd enjoy that very much."

"Not sure it will be enjoyable, but we'll see."

Already, Holly's brain was a-buzz, working on figuring out a way to make the process at least somewhat enjoyable for him. Based on his downcast face, if he needed anything right now, it was a double dose of encouragement and joy.

They were only in the ski instruction area long enough to review all that she'd learned throughout the week. Then Ian faced her with a smile. "Ready to try something a little more challenging?"

She laughed. "That entirely depends on your definition of challenging. If you're planning on pushing me down the tallest and steepest slope here, then the answer is no."

His contagious chortle warmed Holly's heart. Somehow she had to find a way to help him laugh and smile more often.

Ian skied closer. "That's not in my plan. After all, I've already exacted my vengeance on your pushy, entitled behavior on Monday."

"Touché. I admit that I was a little pushy, but pushy with a purpose." And without really thinking through her behavior. "But entitled? Really?"

"Okay, maybe that was just me projecting the behavior of most of my female clientele onto you."

A smirk landed on her face. "Thank you for realizing that possibility. Now that we've cleared that up, and after your promise not to push me down the steepest slope--"

"I don't remember promising."

She sent him a mock glare. "Then let's tackle that subject next, shall we?"

"Okay, I give. I promise not to push you down the steepest slope."

"Or any slope for that matter."

"Yeah, that too."

She offered him a hand to seal the deal. "So, Coach, what did you have in mind?"

He started a slow ski toward the lift on the other side of the lodge, and she fell in beside him. "I thought we'd work on maneuvering the ski lift next, followed by a trip or two down the bunny slope."

Her face lit with a smile, and her spirit soared. "Yay! Do you really think I'm ready?"

"I wouldn't suggest it if I didn't, would I?"

She skewed her lips to one side. "Well..."

He held up a gloved hand. "Okay, don't answer that. But are you going to continue to bring up my poor behavior on Monday?"

"You'd better believe it, Mister."

A few minutes later, they stood near the ski lift, watching other people wait their turn, ski up to the clearing at the right time, and then take a seat as their chair lift arrived.

Evergreen

"See how they turn to look behind them as soon as they get to the landing?"

Holly nodded, a sudden rush of fear pumping adrenaline throughout her system. She breathed in deep to quell both.

Ian looked at her knowingly. "Don't be afraid, Holly. I'll be right there beside you, talking you through the process. And the folks operating the lift are trained to stop the machine if anything goes wrong. You ready to try this?"

She tried to speak, but the words wouldn't come. So instead, she pasted on a grin she didn't feel and gave her head a nod.

In less than three minutes, they were at the point of waiting for the people in front of them to get on the lift. As soon as they headed up to the launch area, Ian, as promised, began talking her through the process, and she followed his instructions. "Okay, Holly, ski to the landing right beside me. Now turn, and watch for the lift. Grab the metal rail, and sit."

Suddenly, they were lifted off the ground, skis dangling below them. Exhilaration quickened her pulse, and she looked around her. Beside them, skiers swooshed from side to side through the snow, practicing their turns. Every once in a while, one would fall and begin the tedious and tiring process of trying to get upright again. But the scenery is what stole her breath away. The bright blue sky, the pure white snow, and especially the miles and miles of evergreen forest that outlined the slope.

"Beautiful, isn't it?"

"Absolutely. I don't think I would ever get tired of this." As much as she loved the city and its hustle and bustle, she always reached the point where she was ready to leave it behind, if only for a short time.

"I feel the same way. I've lived in the area for years now, and I can't see ever wanting to live anywhere else." He paused, then pointed ahead. "We're almost to the top now. Watch these people in front of us. They'll scoot to the front of the seat and carefully angle their skis with the front tips up, so that they can just stand up and ski away when they reach the top."

She watched carefully, her heart once more pounding out an up-tempo rhythm in her chest. How she made it through the process, she had no idea, but she did, and followed Ian around a small curve at the top of the bunny slope.

The grin on his face gave her the same feeling she always got as a school child when she'd done something to please her teachers. "Holly, that was awesome!" He high-fived her.

A grin seemingly permanently engraved on her face disappeared immediately as she stared down the slope in front of her. Uh-oh.

"You okay?"

She swallowed hard. "It didn't look this big from down there."

"You've got this, girl. Just remember your training."

She nodded, but still couldn't slow her pounding heart.

"I'm going to start off, making wide sweeps from side to side. You follow in my tracks. That will keep us from building up too much speed and will also let you practice your turns. Remember--"

"I know, I know. Lean on my downhill ski to make turns."

He grinned. "See? I told you that you had this."

Only after part way down the hill on her first time on the bunny slope, Holly felt herself begin to relax. All her hard work had paid off. No wonder so many people were addicted to snow skiing, though she had no doubt that there were also many who probably gave up on it too quickly. Yes, there was a pretty steep learning curve, but if you prevailed, the rewards were well worth the effort.

Holly was just about to make another right turn when a snow boarder came barreling out of nowhere, and there was no escaping a fall. She did her best to fall the way Ian had taught her, but another person in the mix complicated the whole process. The scream that came out of her mouth took even her by surprise as she landed in a huge bank of snow.

In a flash, Ian was at her side, peering down at her. "You okay?"

She did a quick check. "Well, nothing's hurting. Did that guy leave all my appendages intact?"

"Hmm, let me see. One, two, three. Oops."

"Ha ha. Very funny." Holly pushed herself to a sitting position, so buried in the snow that she could barely see over the side. "Um...any tips for crawling out of a snow bank?"

"Sure. Pack it down." He landed in the bank beside her, then peered over at her. "Sorry, I couldn't let you have all the fun."

For the briefest millisecond, a spark seemed to ignite between them. Thankfully, the moment passed quickly when the offending snowboarder appeared, apologetic. "Dude, I am so sorry."

"For what? Calling me a dude?" Holly brushed off the snow.

"Oh man, you're a girl." He held out a massive gloved hand and helped her to her feet.

Ian rose at the same time, his ski instructor badge dangling from his jacket. "Um...dude, you are aware that this is a beginner's slope and that there are speed restrictions in place, right?"

The guy nodded. "Sorry. I just wasn't paying attention."

"Well, you're lucky that this wasn't a more serious situation. Consider this your warning." His tone was all business. And though he wasn't unkind, he got the point across.

The snowboarder ducked his head. "Yes, sir." He waved and took off down the hill, but this time at a much slower pace.

To clear the tension in the air, Holly attempted to make light of the whole situation. "I'm sure it wasn't intentional."

Ian's eyes, visible because he'd pushed his goggles up on his forehead, took on a hard edge. "It doesn't matter. I had to come down hard on him, Holly. We can't risk him seriously hurting someone just because he wasn't paying attention."

"Guess I didn't think about it like that. Thank you."

"You ready to finish this trip and then do it again?"

She grinned. "Definitely."

As she followed him the rest of the way down, she analyzed the admiration and respect she was beginning to feel for him. Single dad. Thorough teacher. Diligent protector. She gave her head a quick shake. Snap out of it, Holly. After admonishing herself even more, she made a mental note to protect her heart around Ian. It wouldn't do to allow herself those kinds of feelings for a temporary stay in Evergreen.

After her last trip down, she skied over to where Ian stood waiting, his face split with a giant smile.

"You're doing a great job, Holly." His face lost its grin and turned somber. "I...uh, want to apologize again for my stupid stunt on your first lesson. It's no excuse, but I'd had a rough day, was ready to go home, and then you showed up-
-"

"And wouldn't take no for an answer." She smiled. "So I was being just as stupid. For some reason, occasional stupidity seems to be a pretty common trait among us human beings."

He smiled, close-lipped, but didn't break eye contact. "You're being way too easy on me."

The look between them once more reached uncomfortable proportions. Finally Ian nodded toward the lodge and started off in that direction, Holly right behind him.

"So what are your plans for the holidays?"

The question seemed to take him by surprise, and for a long minute he didn't answer. "My plans are to try not to hate Christmas this year."

Holly couldn't control her widening eyes. "What does that mean?" She knew what it meant in her own situation, but were his daughter's problems so bad that he hated Christmas?

"Sorry. Guess I shouldn't have expressed it that way."

"It's totally okay to express what you're feeling, Ian. Don't apologize."

He sighed, his breath visible in the winter air. "Things are just really hard for us right now." They reached the steps leading up to the lodge. Ian began pulling off his skis, so Holly followed suit. He looked her way, his face completely devoid of the earlier joy. "Why don't we meet in the cafeteria in a few minutes for that talk?"

She nodded, a frown hovering over her eyes, as he stomped up the steps and into the lodge.

Holly followed at a distance, her heart in fervent prayer. *Lord, please help Ian and his little girl. Help him to open up to me, and give me wisdom to know what to do and what to say.* A sudden thought interrupted her prayer, causing her to add one more request. *And please help me guard my heart.*

Ian stood in the men's changing room for what seemed like forever, doing what he could to control his racing thoughts, while at the same time trying to make sense of them. Maybe this whole thing with Holly helping Ella was a mistake. He couldn't deny his attraction to her, but she was only here temporarily. Was it wise to ask for her help under those circumstances? It wasn't just his heart at stake here. Ella didn't need to grow attached to someone who would only be gone in a month or so. But what choice did he have?

A heavy sigh pulled air from his lungs, deflating his shoulders. Holly had offered her help. Her credentials appeared to be impeccable. It only made sense, right?

He slammed his locker door a little harder than intended, gathered his bag, and headed upstairs. Waiting and thinking wasn't making this any easier. Better just to talk about it and see where things went from there.

Holly was already waiting when he arrived. She sent a kind smile as he approached.

"Sorry I'm late."

"No worries." Her tone was bright and cheerful. "How's the hot cocoa here? I normally steer clear of sugary drinks, but I want to celebrate my victory over the bunny slope."

He laughed, already feeling more at ease. "It's delicious, especially my special blend." He leaned closer. "I have connections in the kitchen, but you will have to take an oath of secrecy. What happens in the kitchen stays in the kitchen."

She raised her right hand. "Um...okay."

A minute later they entered the kitchen through two stainless steel swinging doors. The kitchen staff looked up, smiling and sending their greetings and smiles Ian's way.

"Don't let us interrupt you. Everyone, this is Holly."

Now his friends greeted her as well.

Ian moved to a less busy part of the kitchen and pulled a few ingredients from the fridge and nearby shelves. "Spices? Check. Almond milk? Check. Organic cacao? Check. Pure maple syrup? Check."

Holly's eyes were wide as she nodded her approval. "I gotta say that I am very impressed with your ingredients' list. They all pass the healthy-for-you test."

In another minute, he had heated the mixture on a gas burner and poured the steaming concoction into two mugs. He pointed to a nearby door. "Let's go that way so we can have a bit more privacy while we talk." She fell into step behind him, and he ushered her into the staff lounge. Good, someone had kept the fire stoked. Just what they both needed after an afternoon in the snow.

"This is nice," announced Holly as she looked around the room.

"Staff lounge. It's usually nice and quiet in here this time of day." He took a seat near the fireplace, stoked the fire, and added a few more logs.

As he took his seat on the sofa next to Holly, he couldn't help but notice the peaceful look on her face as she peered into the flames.

She faced him. "There's nothing like a wood fire. My place in the city has an electric fireplace. It's pretty, but it just can't compare."

"I'm with you there."

Holly blew on her cocoa and took a sip. "Wow, Ian. This is delicious. Have you thought about opening up a hot chocolate stand as a side business?"

"Don't know when I'd have the time. It's about all I can do to hold down this job and keep up with Ella."

"How's she doing?"

He inhaled sharply and lowered his gaze. "Not well." He paused, hoping she'd ask another question, but one glance told him that she was waiting for him to continue. "She seems so depressed and unhappy. Very moody and withdrawn. Yesterday she had a major meltdown, which seems to be happening more and more frequently. I've tried to get through to her, to get her to open up to me, but she's just so different."

"Losing her mom has surely been a traumatic experience for her."

He nodded. "For both of us, but it's like she's getting worse instead of better. I really thought it would be the other way around. That time would soften the blow." He paused again, hoping she'd volunteer information. But she didn't. "I'd really like to get your take on it."

She frowned, but didn't answer.

"I mean, I know you're here for a working vacation, and I'm sure you're busy. But...uh, the other day you offered to help--"

"And that offer still stands."

Relief flooded through him. "Good. Can you tell me how much you charge?"

A light flickered in her eyes, and a tiny smile played on her lips. "Tell you what, if you'll continue to teach me how to ski, I'll do what I can to help Ella in return. And we'll call it even."

Another boulder lifted from his shoulders. Not having more bills to pay was a definite plus. "I like that plan a lot. Thank you." He took a sip of the hot liquid, allowing it to soothe his frayed nerves. "So what do we do from here?"

"Well, I'll need to meet with Ella. I'd like to spend considerable time with her at first. I want her to get to know me so that she feels comfortable confiding in me."

He nodded, but couldn't help the frown that worked onto his face.

"Is that a problem?"

Man, she didn't miss a thing. "No. It's just that I'm fearful of her getting attached to you, and then you leaving."

"I've considered that as well." She sighed. "It is what it is, but I want you to know that I'll be as careful as possible." Sincerity shone from her eyes.

"I believe you, but it's still scary to me."

"For me, as well." She pressed her lips together and lowered her gaze, lost in thought. Finally she raised her head to meet his gaze. "I want to talk about a few things that might not be comfortable for either one of us. But they need to be said."

"Okay. I have some things that I feel like need to be addressed as well."

"Fair enough. First off, no matter how hard it is, if we disagree on something concerning Ella, we need to discuss it privately so that we can present a united strong front to her."

Sounded just like how he and Amy had tried to parent her. "I'm good with that."

"Secondly, we've got to keep the lines of communication open and be completely honest with one another, even if it's uncomfortable."

Relief poured through him. Well, that should make what he needed to say easier. At least maybe a little. "Agreed."

"And last of all, I'm going to need to spend some time with you as well." Discomfort etched every inch of her face, but she continued to plow forward, obviously intent on doing her job. "You may not want to hear this, but you probably have some issues that I could help you with as well. And you and Ella are inextricably linked. You won't be able to help her until you also find help for your own healing."

His mouth gaped open.

"Did I say something wrong?"

Ian snapped out of his daze and shook his head. "No. It's just that Ella said something very similar." As in almost word-for-word.

"She sounds like a very bright girl."

"She is. Smart as a whip. Normally she's a straight-A student, but her grades are slipping. Her last report card had two Fs."

Concern clouded Holly's pretty eyes. "Sounds like we have our work cut out for us. But that's okay. We're headed in the right direction."

Her positive attitude was proving to be just the therapy he needed, at least in this case. Ian raised his cup. "Yes we are. Here's to helping Ella."

Holly clinked her mug against his. "Here's to helping Ella *and you*."

He took a sip of his hot chocolate, suddenly very aware of his own fears and vulnerability. But if it helped Ella, it would be more than worth his own discomfort and unease.

"Now what were your concerns?" She laid her shoulders back as though preparing to do battle.

Why were his knees shaking? He sat down his cup and leaned his elbows on his knees, searching for words. "Please take this in the spirit in which it's intended."

Her face clouded, but she didn't speak.

"I know that being a positive person has its benefits, but the last thing I want is for Ella to get bowled over by a bunch of pep talk that does absolutely nothing to help her."

Hurt landed in her eyes and ensuing anger tightened her features. "Depressed people often need to change their thinking patterns by replacing negative thinking with a more positive outlook. That's just part of how I operate."

He lowered his gaze to his steepled fingers. The last thing he wanted or needed to do was to make her angry, but wasn't this part of the communication she'd mentioned just a few minutes ago? "I get that, but sometimes I wonder if you're for real. You always seem so upbeat that it almost feels phony to me."

"Do I look upbeat and phony to you right now?"

He shook his head.

"I'm a real person, Ian, with real feelings and real problems. But I've learned through my own particular trials to do what I have to do when I get down in the dumps. That includes changing my thinking. It works for me, and I've seen it work for my clients." She clamped her lips together and stared at him hard for what seemed like an eternity, then turned to gather her things. "I'm not sure we are ever going to agree on this point, so it might be best to just call it off now."

Ian jumped to his feet. "Holly, please, I'm sorry. I don't mean to be contentious or make you angry. Ella and I desperately need your help. I'm just struggling to believe if you're for real. And for the sake of my little girl, I need you to be for real. I need you to not just preach, but to live out what you preach. Not just for my sake, but for Ella."

She sat there, her things gathered in a pile on her lap, staring into the fire, the wheels in her brain obviously churning based on the myriad of expressions that passed across her face. Finally she looked up at him. "I'm sorry if I over-reacted. I'm just not used to people questioning my authenticity. I will definitely give your concerns about myself further consideration."

That response alone raised her authenticity a couple of notches in his estimation. Her ability to control herself and concede when she was hurt and angry proved that she had good character.

Holly rose to her feet. "When I get home, I'll look at my schedule and give you a call to set up an appointment."

"Sounds like a plan."

She turned to exit the room, but then turned back his way. "Oh, and I won't be able to do lessons for the next couple of days at least."

Nothing could stop the frown that took up residence on his face as she turned and left the room. While they'd made steps in the right direction for Ella, Ian couldn't help but feel like that in Holly's estimation he had just taken a couple of steps down the ladder.

Five

Holly groggily cracked open one eye. Based on the darkness of the room, it must still be dark outside. She rolled over to check the time.

Ugh. Only 3:30?

In an attempt to get comfortable, she rolled over to try yet another position as she had all night long. Why was it that she could stay on top of her life so well until someone put her in a position where she felt attacked and put on the spot? Ian's words had replayed in her brain all night long. Had she gotten any sleep at all?

All her usual tricks to fall back asleep had been employed. Lavender on her pillow. Breathing deep. Attempting to clear her mind.

But absolutely nothing worked, and she found her brain once more replaying the same old soundtrack of Ian's words. Though he hadn't spoken them in a mean way and was just trying to express his viewpoint, the words had stung. She checked the clock again. 4:00 a.m.

Holly released a disgusted sigh through her nose, feeling totally defeated. There was still one more thing to try, and it involved getting out of bed. A sudden thought made her laugh in derision. Oh, the irony. He'd questioned her ability to practice what she preached, and here she was, doing the very things she advised her patients to do.

Of course, nothing was foolproof. Nine times out of ten, her strategies worked. Just because they weren't working at the minute didn't mean they were a failure. Did it?

She threw back the covers, pulled on her footy socks and robe without turning on a bright light. With the help of her flashlight, she located her Bible and made her way to a comfy chair in the living room. Reading key verses always did the trick when nothing else worked, and how she hoped it worked this time. She wasn't sure her self-esteem could handle it if it didn't work. And the last thing she needed was to take on clients like Ian and Ella when her own doubts and fears were at play.

As she read through favorite verses that brought so much comfort, she felt her inner angst start to subside, replaced by God's peace that was beyond all understanding. She closed her eyes. *Thank You, Lord for Your Word, Your Presence, and Your amazing peace. Help me to do a better job of reaching for Your Word immediately. And help me to let go of the need to be perfect and admired and understood by everyone. Thank You for showing me this facet of myself so I can serve you and others better.*

A yawn worked its way from her mouth. She stretched, feeling suddenly relaxed and sleepy. In a matter of seconds, she was back in bed, snuggling under the covers, and soon thereafter, she drifted off to sleep.

The sun streaming in the windows brought on a gentle awakening. She roused and looked at the clock. 8:30? That never happened. Her first response was to go into panic mode, since her plans for the day were now way behind schedule. But she gave her head a shake, and thanked the Lord for the good rest instead.

In a few minutes' time, she was out the back door, headed for the nearby trail beside the river for her morning exercise. Though the air was cold and frosty, she relished its clean freshness. What she wouldn't give to have a few bottles of this air in New York City. Though she loved the city, it was definitely not one of the healthiest places to live.

The half-frozen river sang out a gurgling song that joined the wind blowing through the tops of the pines. Her heart burst into song in response. "Thank You, God, for the beauty of Your creation."

"Agreed."

The unexpected voice behind her made her jump. She swung around, hands to her chest. "Oh, Ian, you scared me!"

"Sorry. Didn't mean to startle you."

"No. It's okay. I just need to be paying more attention, especially with mountain lions in the area."

His head cocked to one side. "You look really tired. Feeling okay?"

While his thoughtfulness was touching, it was all she could do to keep from pointing the blame back at him. "I just didn't sleep all that great last night."

He grimaced. "Was it because of our conversation? If it was, I'm so sorry. I didn't mean to hurt you. Just trying to practice some of that communication you mentioned. Obviously, I didn't handle it well at all. Please forgive me."

Holly's eyes had grown wider with each word. "I'm not sure I've ever heard you string that many words together at one time."

Ian laughed. "Apology and eating crow don't come easily for me, so I tend to gush a bit."

She resumed her brisk walk, and Ian fell into step beside her. She turned her head his way. "So I gather you live nearby?"

He pointed to the tiny cabin she'd admired the first day she arrived in Evergreen, the one that sat right beside her house-sitting gig. "That's our little tiny cabin right there."

"I love that place. It's so picturesque and perfect."

"We certainly think so. I built that place when I first started my adult life, before Amy and I even met."

Holly raised her eyebrows. "Okay, I'm officially impressed. I don't know that I've ever met someone who physically built their own house."

He shrugged off her complement. "It's not that impressive. It was just something I always wanted to do."

To avoid being overly impressed with him, Holly rushed into her next comment. "I looked at my schedule last night. Since I live here, I think I can make your appointment so that it fits your work schedule and Ella's school schedule."

"Thanks. That would be wonderful. Don't know if you work on the weekends or not, but we have this afternoon open."

"Actually that would be perfect. I do have some writing and other client meetings to prep for, but I can do that whenever. What does Ella like to do? I think it will help her open up if she's just chatting with me while doing whatever she enjoys."

"She used to enjoy a lot of things. Now its hit or miss, based on her mood. Drawing, fishing, hiking, biking. Would any of those work?"

"Possibly. I really need to be around her in her environment. I don't want to ask too many questions this first time out. I just want to get to know her and let her get to know me."

He nodded. "I like that approach. She's the kind of kid who shuts down when she feels pressured. Or at least that's how she's been here of late. So if you could come at it from a friendly perspective, I think that will go a long way with her."

"Good to know. What activity do you suggest for this afternoon?"

"Well, it's supposed to be a pretty day. What if we pick you up after lunch and head to one of our favorite winter hiking spots?"

Holly smiled. Yes, it was perfect. A chance to get to know them both better, see them interact, and take in a beautiful day in the mountains.

Later that day, true to his word, Ian knocked on Holly's door.

She hurried to answer his knock, grabbing her backpack and jacket on the way. But she was totally unprepared for the way her heart skipped a beat when she opened the door to see him smiling at her.

"Ready for this?"

"Definitely." She peered around him at his Subaru, still running in the driveway. "Is she looking forward to the day?"

"Hard to tell. One minute she was packing her backpack like she was. But then in the next minute she was asking if she had to go."

Holly made a face. "Do you think it's because I'm going?"

He shrugged. "Don't have a clue."

"Okay. We'll just do the best we can." She pulled the door shut behind her.

As they neared the vehicle, Holly reached for the passenger door handle. To her surprise, Ian beat her to it and opened the door. She glanced up at him, eyes wide.

"Sorry. It's just the way I was raised."

"That's wonderful. But sadly I'm just not used to it. So please forgive me if I reach for the door handle out of habit."

Holly scooted into the seat while Ian closed her door and moved to the driver's side. She turned toward the backseat. "I know I met you the other day when your dad came to check the internet for me, but I was kind of in panic mode at the time. Sorry I wasn't a better hostess."

"It's okay. My dad's the same way when he's in a hurry." Both her face and her tone held a lackluster quality. As though she'd rather be getting a root canal than to be here.

Well, some response was better than none. Holly smiled at Ian. "So Ella, what's this place like that you're taking me to? The first day I met your dad he tried to kill me, so I'm a little nervous about going on a hiking trip with him anywhere nearby."

The girl's eyes opened wider. "He really tried to kill you?"

Ian shook his head and peered into the rearview mirror. "No, I didn't. She was being pushy and bossy, and I was just trying to teach her a lesson."

Okay, time for a little verbal self-defense. "It was my first time to ski, and he got me the fastest skis he could find. Then he had me do the snowplow without telling me that I needed to be facing downhill. I was actually skiing backward and had no way to stop."

With each word of the story, Ella laughed harder and harder, holding her sides.

"Oh, and then he neglected to tell me how to fall until I had already fallen! Sheesh, what kind of teacher are you anyway?"

The girl stopped laughing long enough to agree. "Yeah, Dad. You need to work on your teaching skills a bit."

Holly took in Ian's pasted-on smile that didn't reach his eyes. Oops, time to do some damage control. "In all fairness, I deserved it. I was pretty rude and demanding and late. Your dad's really a great teacher. I actually made it down the bunny slope a few times yesterday."

Ian's granite-hard face softened. "Well, I'm glad we at least ended on the good part. Though you could have totally left out the part about me trying to kill you."

Ella protested. "But that was the funniest part. I just have this picture in my head of Holly going down the hill backwards." Her giggle resumed.

Ian peered at his daughter in the rearview mirror. "The funniest part was when she threw up."

Ella's face lost its merriment. "That's not funny at all." She looked over at Holly. "Let me guess. Altitude sickness?"

"Yeah. Something else he forgot to mention. But I can finally breathe up here now. Progress!" She did a fist pump that brought forth another giggle from Ella. "But I really do want to know about this trail."

Ella's face grew animated. "It's really cool. It takes a while to hike it in the snow, but when you get to the overlook and look down into the valley, especially on a sunny day like today, it's totally worth it. You can see for miles and miles."

Holly did a pretend whisper over the back seat. "Will you promise to stand between me and your dad so that he won't push me over the side of the mountain?"

Ella laughed out loud. "I promise."

The rest of the drive up was fun and lighthearted. They all participated in the conversation, and the talk ranged from school to New York City and to Ian's work as a ski instructor and firefighter.

Holly's interest ratcheted up another notch at this latest tidbit of information. "You're really a firefighter?"

"Yeah, really."

"But how do you have time when you're a ski instructor?"

Another infectious giggle sounded from the backseat. "Well, the two jobs don't overlap, you know."

Holly did a palm plant to her forehead. Well, duh. "Silly me. Guess you can't have snow and forest fires at the same time."

"Technically, it could happen under special circumstances, but I've never seen it happen here. Usually we have a monsoon season between our fire season and snow season."

Holly couldn't help the derisive laugh that escaped her lips. "Monsoon? In Colorado?"

"He's telling the truth," chimed in Ella. "Sometimes we call it the rainy season, but during July and August, it's not unusual for us to get rain every afternoon."

For a while, the conversation died down, giving Holly time to contemplate what a surprise and downright enigma Ian was turning out to be. Yes, he needed some help in learning to communicate better with his daughter, but there was no doubt that the two loved each other. Somehow, she had to find a way to bridge the gap between them. "Ella, what are you hoping to get for Christmas?"

The silence elongated so long, Holly started scrambling for a way to change the subject, but finally Ella answered. "Maybe you should ask my dad that question."

Holly skewed her lips to one side. Okay, note to self. Christmas was a sore point between them. Not only had Ella gone completely silent, Ian now had a huge scowl on his face.

Thankfully, the taut silence didn't last much longer. Within a few minutes they arrived at the trail head and parked. Holly climbed from the Subaru in utter awe. The evergreens here towered taller than any she'd seen so far, including at the ski basin. "These trees are enormous."

Ian came to stand beside her, donning his jacket and zipping it up. "You haven't seen anything yet, has she, Ella?"

The girl stepped up on the other side of Holly, also pulling on her coat. "Nope. They get even taller as we get close to the top. Dad, where are the snowshoes?"

"Back of the Subaru."

"Snowshoes? Um...I though we were hiking."

The humor on his face proved that he found her comment comical. "We are, but when you hike in snow this deep and in a place where there's not a lot of foot traffic this time of the year, you need them."

"Are they anything like skis?"

Ian smirked at her moment of panic. "No need to worry. They're completely safe." He moved toward the vehicle to help Ella, and Holly joined them.

But it quickly became apparent that Ella wasn't happy. She swatted at tears on her face, then faced Ian with both arms ramrod straight and fists clenched. "These snowshoes are Mom's."

"I know, honey, but I didn't think you'd mind if Holly borrowed them."

Okay, she had to somehow diffuse the situation. "It's okay, Ella. I won't use them if you don't want me to. I really prefer to hike in my boots instead anyway."

Ian started to protest, but Holly sent him a 'don't-do-it' look.

Ella stood there silently, her head lowered, obviously doing battle with her feelings. Finally she turned and handed the snowshoes to Holly. "You can't hike in snow this deep without snowshoes. It would be too dangerous. You might disappear in a snowdrift."

"Well, I wouldn't want to do that. Oh, wait, I did that yesterday on the ski slope when that crazy snow boarder thought he was a bowling ball and I was a pin."

Ella's sad face completely disappeared, replaced by a bright cheery smile and a giggle. "Remind me to go snow skiing with you sometime. I'd probably die laughing."

Now Ian laughed. "She is pretty funny to watch."

"Okay, okay, enough poking fun at me. Who's going to show me how to attach these over-sized tennis rackets to my feet?" Within in a matter of minutes, Ella and Ian had Holly geared up and ready to go.

Now that the mood had once more lightened, Holly opted to just enjoy the scenery and pay attention to how Ella and Ian interacted, only joining in from time to time. It didn't take long for her suspicions to be confirmed. First off, the two truly loved each other, but their individual takes on the loss of their loved ones were contradicting each other. Secondly, Ella vacillated between being a happy-go-lucky little girl and a moody pre-teen, which would require a close look at her diet and other factors. Last of all, Ian--though well-intentioned and with his heart in the right place--struggled immensely with knowing how to be both mother and father to his hurting little girl, and understandably so.

And it was there that she had to enter into the situation with trepidation and trembling. Because of Ella's personality and hurt, she could potentially latch on to Holly like a buoy in stormy seas. But how would that scenario play itself out, especially when her time here was up and it was time to return to the city?

❄

His heart full beyond measure at the surrounding beauty and the way things were playing out, Ian led the way up the trail, Ella behind him and Holly taking up the caboose position. His thoughts lingered on Holly. She was better than he'd even dared hope for. On more than one occasion she'd managed to lighten tense situations with Ella and turn things around before they disintegrated and ruined the whole day.

Now they were in one of his favorite places, Ella chatting away like a happy little bird. But the best part was that this was the closest to normal that they'd been since Amy's death.

The trail took a sharp turn to the right. "Here's the last switchback."

"What's a switchback?" Holly's word sounded from behind Ella.

Ella jumped in with the answer before he could. "It's how the trail zigzags going up and down the mountain. If we didn't have switchbacks, the mountain would be too steep to climb."

Ian couldn't help but smile at Ella's perfect description, but everything about this moment felt right. It wouldn't be long now until they'd be at the top. Already the trail was widening and more sky came into view--the perfect parallel to all that he and Ella had been going through.

It had been an uphill climb for both of them, and sometimes it seemed like they went downhill rather than up. But with Holly's help, it felt like they were finally on the right track. As though the trail through the aftermath of Amy's death was widening and becoming easier to traverse. And most especially that the sky was brightening after so many days of confusing darkness.

"Here we are, ladies." Ian took a step off to one side, so Ella and Holly could step in beside him to take in the view. "Watch your step. It's probably slippery in places." He grinned over at Holly. "And in spite of your belief that I have it in for you, I really don't want those slippery spots to make us lose you."

Her smile faded, and then partially returned, a growing look of discomfort on her face.

He once more faced the view, berating himself for the way the words had come out of his mouth, echoing what was already in his heart. Had he actually used the phrase, 'lose you?' Really?

Ella snuggled up next to his side and wrapped both arms around him. "Oh, Daddy, it's so beautiful. I think I must've forgotten exactly how gorgeous this place is." She tilted her head back to smile up at him. "Thank you for bringing us here."

He stooped low and planted a kiss on the top of her hair, breathing in the precious scent of his little girl and breathing out gratitude for this shining moment. "You're welcome, sweetheart. Thank you for coming with me. Having a good time?"

Her face contorted with a confusing mix of emotions, but she nodded. "Yes. Holly's really funny."

Ian sent an amused glance Holly's way.

She shrugged and smirked. "That's me. Comic relief."

That and so much more. If only she knew how much more. Ian gulped in a big breath of fresh air and once more focused on the view, doing all he could to keep his footing on a very slippery slope. One he wasn't sure his heart could take. To refocus his attention elsewhere, he shrugged off his backpack, then brushed the snow from a nearby boulder that was totally encased in sunshine. "You guys want some snacks?"

Ella clapped her mittens together. "Yay! A picnic. I'm starving!"

"Count me in." Holly laid a hand on her stomach. "There's something about being out in the fresh mountain air that makes me ravenous. Same thing happens with skiing."

Ian unzipped his backpack and pulled out three stainless steel cups full of water. Next he retrieved the peanut butter sandwiches he'd made that morning before they left.

Holly peered over at his menu items, then shrugged off her own backpack and started unloading items. "Hope you don't mind, but I also brought food."

"The more the merrier."

Ella made a beeline to Holly. "What did you bring?"

"Walnuts and almonds." She handed Ella the bag, and then reached into her backpack again. "Homemade granola."

Ian's eyebrows shot upward. Wow, she was totally showing him up.

Holly once more dug in her bag. "Along with plain yogurt mixed with berries and cinnamon."

Ella grabbed for the bowls. "I love berries and yogurt and cinnamon."

Holly grinned at Ian and offered him a bag of granola. "Want some?"

He took it. "Thanks. You eat healthy, I see."

"I had to learn how, but I wouldn't have it any other way."

He cocked his head to one side. "Why?"

"Because of some traumatic events, I fell into a really bad bout of depression. Then I had a major wake-up call with my health, which forced me to examine every aspect of my life and make the necessary changes."

So she really was the person she claimed to be online. The next thought brought a bad taste to his mouth. And she was trying to practice what she preached, despite his assertions to the contrary. No wonder she'd been so upset yesterday at their post-ski lesson meeting.

They all took a seat in the sunshine atop the huge boulder with their feast spread out in front of them. Within a few seconds, Holly and Ella were chatting like they'd known each other their entire lives. Gratitude flooded Ian's whole being.

Later, as they packed up to head down the trail, Ian managed to find the opportunity to express his gratitude to Holly. She had just zipped up her backpack when he stepped up to her. He intentionally kept his voice low to keep from capturing Ella's attention, who sat a few feet away from them, back turned, as she peered out over the sun-dappled valley below. "Holly, words can't express how grateful I am for your help. You're nothing short of a miracle-worker."

Her face lit from within, and she grabbed his hand. "I'm not sure I'd go that far, but I'm always happy to help in whatever way I can."

The invisible spark between them once more returned, and it was as though they were frozen in this particular moment, unable to break their hands or eyes away from the other. Then Ian sensed someone other than himself and Holly. Ella! He yanked his gaze and his hand away from Holly and turned to face his daughter.

Her arms were crossed in front of her chest and the blackest of angry winter storms had taken a position on her face. She snatched up her backpack and stormed down the trail ahead of them.

Holly's face paled considerably. "I'm so sorry."

"Don't be. It's not your fault."

The two of them set out at a quick pace to keep up with Ella, who was quickly disappearing from view.

"I just hope I didn't undo all that was accomplished in the past few hours." Both Holly's face and her tone revealed just how distraught she was.

"Don't blame just yourself." Typical of his life over the past two years. One step forward and then two steps back.

Holly frowned. "She's pulling away from us. Do we need to pick up the pace?" Already her breath was labored and coming in spurts.

A battle erupted in Ian's head. "Debating that very thing. Ella knows the way down by herself. She's grown up in this environment and knows what to do in case of an emergency. But when she gets in these moods of hers, all good judgment seems to fly out the window." He looked over at Holly. "If I leave a good trail, can you follow it?"

"Absolutely. I'd feel much better if you could go after her. I'm just holding you back."

He smiled his appreciation. "Thank you." In a flash he was off, half-walking, half-running, wishing for just this once that he could ditch the snowshoes.

As he got further down the mountain, Ian started calling. "Ella! Wait up!" Every once in a while, he thought he caught glimpse of her navy toboggan with the puffy tassel on top or her Christmas red scarf, but then just as quickly, that glimpse would disappear.

Fear unlike any he'd ever known erupted inside, sending icy tentacles to squeeze his lungs and steal his breath. His mind followed suit, instantly imagining all that could go wrong. A fall. Getting off the trail. Getting lost in the snowy forest. Mountain lions. But he didn't dare stop. He pressed down the mountain as fast as his legs and the steep trail would allow, his lungs pleading for more air, his heart pleading for God's mercy, and his mouth calling her name, over and over again.

But when he reached the Subaru, and with absolutely no sign of Ella, his fear quadrupled. "Ella! Ella!" Ian cupped his hands around his mouth and yelled her name in several different directions. He reached for his phone, not entirely surprised to find that he had no signal. He peered up at the quickly-darkening sky. Though it was still afternoon, snow clouds had rolled in. Couple that with the fact that the sun was now on the other side of the mountain, with night-time freezing temps descending, and you had a recipe for disaster. Now what?

The answer came immediately. He had no choice but to continue to search the area for Ella. He'd retrace his steps and maybe find a spot where Ella had veered from the trail, find Holly, and send her down the mountain until she could get a cell phone signal. Then she could call 911 and get search and rescue underway.

Ian hadn't made it very far up the trail until Holly spotted him and came running toward him. "Did you find her?"

He shook his head, doing all he could to maintain the calm needed for this type of situation. "And we also can't get a cell phone signal up here."

"What can I do to help?"

The concern on her face warmed him from the inside out. She always wanted to help. Like that was her mission in life. "I need you to take the Subaru down the hill until you get a phone signal. Then call 911 and tell them what's happened and that we're up at the Verde Peak Overlook Trail."

She nodded, her face growing more pale by the second.

"You okay with this?"

Though her face said otherwise, she nodded adamantly.

He handed her the keys. "I'm going to backtrack all the way back up the mountain if needed. Maybe I can find a place where she veered off the trail. You honk the horn when you get back up."

She nodded again, her eyes wide with fear, then turned to hurry down the hill to the parking lot below.

Ian again glanced up at the bluish-black clouds, just as the wind picked up and big, chunky snowflakes began to fall.

Six

"I can do this. God is with me." Holly repeated the words over and over again as she ran through the enormous blowing snowflakes, removed her snowshoes, and climbed into the Subaru. She hastily checked the layout of everything on the dashboard, steering wheel, and gear shift. Not much resemblance to the Jeep she'd rented, but she'd have to make it work. She located the 4-wheel drive button, but then realized she had no idea how to engage it. And there just wasn't time to sit and read the owner's manual.

She started the car and the wipers, then raised her gaze upward as she put the gear into reverse. "Lord, help us all."

Already the snow had covered the pavement. The only thing that made it possible for Holly to see where to drive was the trees and guardrails on either side. Each turn and each spot of downhill or uphill driving ratcheted up her fear another notch.

Holly found a flat spot, braked to a stop, and checked her phone for a signal. Still nothing.

She started down yet another steep hill. Wait! Was that Ella's scarf? She blinked hard, trying her best to see despite the blowing snow, wipers, and ever-approaching darkness.

A breeze stirred, whipping the scarf from side to side. That had to be Ella's scarf. With the snow and overcast skies, she could have easily missed it. Inhaling sharply to hopefully quell her fear, Holly tried to brake slowly, but with the ever-thickening snow, her wheels took on a mind of their own. In slow motion, the car careened off the road to the right and landed on a downward slope, precariously perched with the nose of the vehicle against a tree.

There was no time to try to get the vehicle unstuck now. Not if that scarf belonged to Ella.

She jumped from the Subaru. Immediately her eyes stung from both the wind and blowing snow, making it even more difficult to find her way across the road to the scarf. But bit by bit, the scarf grew closer. Hope burgeoned in her chest. Yes, that was definitely Ella's scarf!

"Ella! Ella!" The wind seemed to catch her words and carry them away as a whisper.

"Holly!" The voice was faint, but it appeared to be coming from beyond where the scarf still whipped back and forth in the wind.

"Ella! Where are you?"

"Down here. Don't get too close. I slipped and fell."

Out of pure instinct, Holly fell to all fours and inched in the direction of the voice. "Keep talking to me, sweetie. I'm trying to crawl toward you."

"I'm over here." The girl started crying--loud, heartbreaking sobs. But at least there was enough sound that Holly could hear her.

After what seemed like an eternity, she reached the edge of the road, only inches from where the guardrail started. "Okay, Ella, I'm right above you. Are you hurt?"

"My ankle might be sprained, but other than that, I think I'm okay."

Ropes. They needed ropes. "Honey, do you know if your dad keeps rope in your car?"

"Yes, he does. He always says that you never know when you might need them in the winter. Where is he?"

"He was headed back up the trail to look for you, and I came down the road to hopefully get cell phone service to call 911."

The girl's sobs started in again. "This is all my fault. I want my Daddy to be okay."

A sudden peace descended over Holly. "Your dad is a strong man, Ella. I have no doubt that he's okay. So now I need you to be strong and brave so we can go back and get him, okay?"

The sobs subsided to a few sniffles. "Okay."

"I'm going back to the car for the rope. We'll use this guard rail to pull you up."

"Great plan." Ella's voice now held confidence instead of fear.

Carefully, Holly rose to her feet and made her way back across the road. Thankfully, she'd left the head lamps on so the Subaru was easy to spot, even in the bad weather. In addition to the ropes, Holly also found a heavy duty flashlight. "Thank You, Lord that Ian keeps his vehicle prepared for emergencies."

In only a few minutes' time, Holly was back at the guard rail. "I'm back, Ella. I'm tying a loop for you to put under your arms. After you do that, I want you to cinch the rope as tight as you can and tie all the knots you can."

"Got it."

Holly threw the loop over the side. "Now I'm running my end of the rope over and around the guardrail. You'll need to use your feet against the cliff and your arms to pull."

"I think I can handle it. Dad and I sometimes go rock climbing, so I know what to do."

A sigh of relief gushed from Holly's mouth, and she once more breathed a prayer of thanksgiving that Ian and Holly knew what to do in these situations, even if she didn't. "Okay. Let me know when you're ready for me to pull."

"I'm ready."

A moment of panic at what she was about to try to do sent Holly's whirring brain into a tailspin. All the potential pitfalls flashed through her mind. "Are you sure you tied the knots really tight?"

"I'm sure."

Holly breathed in deep, praying. "Okay. Here we go." She tugged on the rope and felt Ella's weight lift off the ground.

"It's working!" Ella's voice held excitement. "Keep pulling."

"I am, but you hold on to that rope, okay?" She pulled again, almost slipping in the snow, with the same results. Careful not to let the rope slip, Holly pointed the flashlight in the direction of the rope. Already there was a slight fray. Her prayers grew more fervent with each pull of the rope.

Finally after about ten pulls, Ella waved a hand up in the air, catching the beam of light from the flashlight that Holly had placed on the ground.

"We're almost there!" Ella's voice held excitement.

But now what? Somehow she had to get closer to the guardrail and tie off the rope without letting Ella slip back down. "Okay. I'm just trying to think through what to do next."

"Take the rope in one hand and start making loops in the rope--like you're rolling up a lasso--as you get closer to the railing. But keep the rope pulled taut."

"Okay." Holly took a step toward the guard rail, but as she did so, the rope slipped and Ella dropped.

The little girl screamed and once more began crying.

Heart in her throat and pounding furiously, Holly leaned her weight backward to keep the rope taut. "It's okay, Ella." Holly did all she could to keep her voice calm, but it still held a frightened tremor. Hopefully Ella couldn't detect her fear. "I'm going to raise you back up and then try again, so hold on."

"Okay, but please don't drop me."

The fearful plea tugged at Holly's heart. She looked into the descending snow flakes and cried out to God, lifted

Ella back to her previous position, and then tried again to move closer to the guard rail. This time it worked. Holly breathed out a sigh of relief.

"You did it." Ella stopped crying.

Holly repeated the process over and over again until she stood near the guardrail.

"Now just tie it off and pull me up the rest of the way." Only a smidgen of fear sounded in Ella's voice.

Holly followed the instructions, and the procedure went off without any problems. Within minutes, Ella was safely standing on solid ground, crying and hugging Holly.

All Holly could do for the first few minutes was to fall to the ground with Ella in her arms and cry out the emotions that had built up inside. "I was so afraid, Ella."

Ella hugged her tighter. "It's okay, Holly."

The simple words worked, and she was able to regain her composure.

Ella pulled away to send a sweet smile. "Thank you for saving me, but can we please go find my Daddy?"

Ian paced back and forth in the parking area at the trail head, his snow shoes in his hands. Where was Holly? What was taking so long? He'd already been up the trail two more times, with absolutely no sign that Ella had veered from the path. And he'd had lots of time to think through every scenario. And he could only reach one logical conclusion. Ella wouldn't have veered from the trail. Hadn't he pounded the rule about never leaving the trail into that head of hers?

No, it was far more likely that she kept walking down the road.

At just that moment, he heard a faint noise, like that of a little girl screaming. Was that Ella? Or maybe a mountain lion?

He took off in the direction of the road, traveling as fast as possible. Though it was still snowing hard, since the parking lot and road had been plowed prior to the snow, the accumulation was only a few inches deep.

Then he heard it. Faintly at first, but with each step down the road, the sound grew louder. A car horn.

He picked up the pace, careful to stay in the middle of the road. It was almost dark by this point, but there was still enough light to barely see down the road.

As he topped a hill and looked down, he could make out the lights of a vehicle off to the right and shining on a bunch of trees. The Subaru.

He made his way down the hill half-sliding, half-running, his pulse and thoughts racing. Was Holly injured? Had she been unable to get a cell phone signal? And where was Ella? His eyes swam with unshed tears, making it difficult to see.

Finally he reached the Subaru, quickly brushing snow from the driver's side window and pounding at the same time. Holly jumped from the car and into his arms. Then, unexpectedly, the back door opened and Ella joined them. They all sank to the ground, crying and holding tightly to one another.

Finally Ian pulled away from Ella and Holly, swiping tears from his face and holding up a hand to stop the chatter that erupted from both of them. "I really do want to hear the story, but we need to get the car unstuck before it gets any darker." He headed to the front of the vehicle to assess the damage, and then walked all the way around it. "I don't think there's any damage."

"I tried to get it out after I found Ella, but it wouldn't budge.

"Let's try again with me and Ella pushing."

Holly nodded and jumped back in the driver's seat. She started the ignition and put the car in reverse.

"On the count of three, we'll push while you give it just a little gas. Don't floor it or we could get stuck even worse."

"Okay."

"One. Two. Three."

Just as he'd instructed, she gently applied the gas while he and Ella threw their weight against the front of the car. But the car didn't budge even a little bit.

He moved to the driver's side window, motioning for Ella to join him. "Try again, but this time I want to check out the back tires."

She tried again while he and Ella watched the tires, both careful to stay out of the way.

On the passenger side rear wheel he spied the problem. That wheel sat about an inch off the ground, unable to gain any traction. Ian motioned for Holly to stop, then opened the tailgate and retrieved one of the boards he kept in the vehicle for situations like this. He wedged it under the tire and then motioned for Holly to try again. At first, it looked like nothing would happen, but then, the tire grabbed hold, and Holly easily backed out into the road.

All three erupted in cheers.

As Holly exited the driver's side to move around to the other side, she looked up at Ian. "I've never been so glad to be out of the driver's seat in my life."

He smiled. As she turned to walk away, he reached out and snagged her arm, turning her attention back to him once more. At first he couldn't speak around the over-sized lump in his throat, but he finally managed get the words out as tears filled his eyes. "Thank you for saving Ella's life. Words just aren't enough."

"It was truly all my joy and pleasure. And I couldn't have done it without the Lord's help. He gave me a strength and clear mind that I just can't take credit for."

God? She believed in God? He climbed into the drivers' seat, leaving her standing there for a moment with questions in her eyes, before she finally traipsed through the thick snow to climb in through the passenger side door.

All the way back down the mountain and across the valley to where they lived she spoke not a word. Instead she stared out the window, her lips pursed as though deep in thought.

Only when they reached her house did she speak, and that was more to Ella than to him. Her only comment to him was a perfunctory "Good night."

Seven

Exhausted beyond measure, Holly tried to unwind and take her mind off the events of the day, but her efforts failed. It was as if the harder she tried not to think about Ian's hardened face when she'd mentioned God's name, the more her mind dwelled on it. Of course it didn't help matters that her body was more than likely on adrenaline and cortisol overload from the ordeals of the day.

Okay, Holly, get this out of your system. Address it. Deal with it right here and now and get it over with. A heavy sigh fell from her, deflating her posture and her spirit in one fell swoop.

Why was it that the more she wanted to help people, the more stuff kept getting in the way, including herself?

The answer came immediately. The enemy. He wanted to trip her up and even make her doubt that her efforts to help were actually worthwhile.

But then on top of all that were her own fickle emotions. She could no longer deny that her heart was headed in an unwanted direction when it came to Ian. But even in the darkening light of the mountain side, she'd glimpsed hostility in his face when she mentioned the Lord. So now in addition to the question of how could she help both Ian and Ella and protect her heart at the same time, she questioned how she could have feelings for a non-believer. Hadn't she learned that lesson with Bruce?

Somehow she had to find a way to extricate herself from a very difficult situation before it ballooned to even more epic proportions.

Then a conflicting thought tugged at her heart. Her mind returned to the scene where she and Ella and Ian had stood in the middle of the road, hugging and crying. Like a real family. Tears spilled out of her eyes and slipped down her cheeks. How long had it been since she'd experienced that feeling of family, and how was she supposed to just let it go now that she'd found it again?

Her gaze was suddenly drawn to two index cards poking out from between pages of her Bible. Curious, she reached for them and pulled. The same two verses she'd landed upon when making her decision to come to Evergreen. God's Spirit had so impressed them upon her heart that she'd written them down. Was it pure coincidence that she'd found them again during this particular time of confusion?

Not a chance.

She read them out loud several times, allowing herself to consider not only their meaning, but also how they should impact her actions in this current situation.

Her cell phone buzzed from its kitchen counter location. She rose from the couch and hurried over to it to read the screen.

Ian.

Lord, what do I do?

Answer it. She had to answer it, if for no other reason than to find out how he and Ella were doing. She sent another sentence prayer requesting God's help and wisdom.

"Hello?"

"Hey, Holly. I was starting to wonder if you were going to pick up."

She ignored the comment. "How's Ella?"

"Sleeping like a log. The events of the day pretty much wore her out."

"I can relate."

He chuckled softly. "As can I." He paused. "Was that why you were so quiet on the way home?"

How did she answer that, one, without lying, and two, without moving into an area of conversation for which she was totally unprepared? "That was probably part of it."

"And the other part?"

"I'm actually still trying to figure the rest of it out." That was not a lie. While she might have part of the answer, the rest of it had been interrupted by his phone call.

He sighed, but didn't respond.

Okay, time to change the subject. "How are you doing after such an exhausting day?"

"I think I'm kind of in the same place you are."

Well, so much for changing the subject. Maybe approaching it from a client-based slant would help. "Did you and Ella get a chance to talk through what happened?"

"Yeah. That was definitely the biggest plus to the day. She admitted that she'd gotten mad at me, and that's why she took off."

Every fiber of her being longed to ask him why Ella had gotten mad, but Holly refrained. Best not to open that can of worms. Instead, it was just another puzzle piece she now had to add to the puzzle of finding the answer to her predicament. "Did she express remorse to you?"

"Yeah, she did. Made me so proud that she was upfront with me about her responsibility in the events of the day."

"That definitely shows growth and maturity, which is what we're after."

"So where do we go from here?" The question hung in the air like a hovering storm cloud.

Where indeed? "Um...at some point, I need to speak with you both individually and then together. I feel like it's important that Ella knows at some point that you hired me to help her and not..." How should she finish the statement?

The silence on the other end was deafening, followed by a soft sigh. "...and not anything more than that?"

There. He'd said it. Wrapped up the puzzle and topped it off with a neat and tidy bow. All she had to do was agree. "Yes."

Now the silence between them was excruciating. So much so that Holly felt the need to fill it with some sort of comment. "I'll look at my schedule and then contact you to set an appointment with you and Ella, both individually and together."

"Sounds good. Bye."

As she ended the call, only one thought reverberated in her brain, much like a clanging alarm. Ian's tone had taken on the same detached, business-only tone as hers.

But she had to trust that it was all for the best.

Tuesday morning Holly dragged herself out of bed. Make that two nights in a row where her sleep had suffered. No wonder she had a hankering for a box full of Krispy Kreme doughnuts. Maybe a quick walk would take her mind off her carb cravings. She quickly donned her winter exercise gear and headed out the door. In less than a minute she stood at the trail, looking both ways. Good, no sign of Ian in either direction. She opted to go left this time, since she'd gone right yesterday. That way if he was on the trail looking for her, he was headed in the opposite direction.

At some point she needed to call him back to make those appointments. But for now what she needed more than anything was a respite for her troubled thoughts. She forced her attention to the beauty around her. But after only ten minutes down the path, she spotted Ian jogging toward her. To make matters worse, he saw her as well, because he waved.

Now she had no choice but to keep walking toward him, when her first inclination had been to turn and run in the opposite direction.

He slowed to a stop as he reached her, hands on his hips, smoke rising from his mouth and nose in the cold morning air. "Good morning." His eyes searched her face. "Bad night again?"

Ugh. Was it really that obvious? "Yeah."

He turned and fell into step beside her, since, for reasons she couldn't fully explain, she'd resumed her walk. "Same here."

Holly kept her mouth closed, mainly because she hadn't a clue on how to respond. But somehow she needed to use this opportune time to deal with him as a client. That would save her having to set up an appointment later.

"When I think about all that could've happened yesterday..." His face seemed to age with weary lines right before her eyes.

"Don't be so hard on yourself, Ian. You're doing a great job with Ella. She's just struggling right now." Holly hesitated briefly. "You don't have to be Super Dad. Just be you. You're already a wonderful father."

"Thanks. I try."

"I know you do." She paused to inhale deeply, the cold air burning inside her nose. Would he take what she had to say next in the way she intended it? Well, regardless, it needed to be said. "You know, one thing I noticed yesterday is that you tend to come to her rescue, even in little ways. And I'm not referring to her disappearance. That was the time to come to her rescue."

"You mean coming to her rescue when she needs to learn to cope and deal with things on her own."

"Yes. Every time you come to her rescue, I think it makes her feel like she's incapable of dealing with things on her own. Pretty soon that has a way of becoming a self-fulfilling prophecy."

His mouth gaped open, and he stared at her briefly before re-focusing his attention on the path in front of them.

The silence seemed to last forever, but he obviously needed the time to process her comment and his thoughts.

"I just want to protect her."

"See? More proof that you're a good dad." She paused. "But you have the tendency to rescue her when she doesn't always need you to."

He must have recognized the truth of her words, because he nodded in agreement. "Okay. Note to self: Don't be too quick to rush in and rescue her."

"Right. And give her more age-appropriate freedom. It will help her self-confidence so much. Ella is not only sweet. She's also smart and capable. Give her time. She'll come around."

"That's my Christmas wish."

His choice of words exploded inside Holly like a grenade. It was becoming more and more apparent that his lack of faith in God was going to be a problem, not only in their relationship with each other, but in her ability to help him and Ella. Without God, was there really anything she could do?

Ian broke the silence. "Where are you from anyway? I've tried to detect a recognizable accent, but I quite figure it out."

"I grew up in the Midwest, but now my home base is New York City."

"Why there?"

She shrugged. "I guess because the city has a little bit of everything, which suits me well. But truthfully, I'm somewhat of a nomad." The silence that ensued felt very uncomfortable, because only one thought popped into her mind, and for some weird reason she felt compelled to verbalize it. "Which I guess is just another way of saying that I don't really have a home."

"Do you mind if I ask you another question?" Without waiting for her to answer, he plowed ahead. "Why don't you have a husband or boyfriend to spend the holidays with?"

The words hit with the impact of a sledge hammer. She lowered her head, her mind racing to find the right words. "Uh, I was engaged once, but my boyfriend broke up with me right before Christmas." An anniversary her mind and heart always celebrated without her permission, and one that would once more descend before she was fully ready to wage that war. "So I've been more than a little leery of letting anyone else in."

"Not all guys are jerks, you know. But I'm sure that must've hurt."

"It did." Though it had been for the best, had she really recovered? Darcy would answer to the negative on that one.

"What happened?"

"Turns out we weren't on the same page. Or plan. We'd agreed to a plan for our future, but he decided that he just couldn't handle it."

"You've got my curiosity up. Tell me about this so-called plan."

"Oh, you know. We were going to prolong our engagement for a couple of years so we could both pursue our careers and save for our wedding and a house. It was important to both of us to travel and enjoy life, so we mapped out several vacations as part of our plan." Vacations she'd paid for.

His lips quirked to one side and his eyebrows took a lazy ride up his forehead. "I get the idea of planning ahead, but I'm not sure you can really plan out your future. My life certainly didn't turn out the way I expected."

Good point. Neither had hers. "Yeah, but we wanted to make sure that we were financially prepared for marriage, that we had all our ducks in a row so to speak. And we wanted to take time to get to know each other and not rush into it."

"But doesn't that kind of plan rule out fun and spontaneity and adventure?"

Another good point. Was that why she had taken to traveling the world to hopefully bring those things into her life? "Maybe. But I still think it was important for us to get to know each other." How ironic that getting to know Bruce had actually helped her move on. It was the part after the break-up which had proved to be a wound that might never heal.

Ian continued his stance against making plans. "In my opinion, you can't manipulate life. If you try, you end up manipulating people, and most folks don't appreciate that." He paused. "Based on something you said yesterday, I assume you're a person of faith. It seems to me that making a long-term plan could leave the faith aspect out of the equation, at least to a certain extent."

Holly's mouth fell open, her breathing suspended momentarily. *Oh, Lord, I'm so sorry. I was so busy making plans for the perfect life that I didn't trust in You the way I should have.*

He pointed to a grove of pine trees ahead. "Take those trees for example. They don't make plans. They just do what they were made to do. I wish more people were like that."

"I get what you're saying, but I think there's a way to plan with faith." She stopped and looked at one tree in particular, one that grew out of a boulder. "Look at that one. It's growing out of a rock." It might not make plans, but it did know to send it's roots deep into the water. The verses from Jeremiah and Psalms flooded into her memory, and she made a mental note to look them up again later for further study. "What about your wife? Were you opposites, one a planner like me and the other, well, like you?"

"Thanks for making me sound flawed somehow." He drawled the words out drolly.

"That's not what I meant." Even though he had inadvertently made her feel the same.

"It's okay. As far as our relationship was concerned, we were on the same page. I don't think you should have to work so hard to fall in love. Falling in love with Amy was thrilling and exciting and unpredictable and totally unscripted."

She grimaced. "That sounds terrifying." And totally awesome. "Back to the trees for a minute. Do you know the best places nearby to buy a real Christmas tree?" Already she could imagine the fresh pine scent flooding the house. Hmm, maybe she needed more than just one.

"Most folks who want the real thing go up into the mountains and cut one down. I have some friends that will let us get one from their property for free."

"Where at?"

"The ski basin. Want to go get one right now? It's a perfect day for it." He glanced at his watch. "Ella is almost through with school. We should have time to pick her up, head up the mountain, cut a tree, and get back down by dark."

Clanging alarms went off in her brain. It would be great to get a free tree and get in some more time with Ella. But was it really a wise move to spend even more time with Ian? And could she overcome the temptation to fall in love with the idea of family rather than wait for the one God might have in store?

She sent up a quick prayer, answered immediately with the thought that God was with her. As long as she stayed in step with His Spirit within her, all would be fine. An excitement for Christmas she hadn't experienced in such a long time erupted inside, taking her by surprise. She grinned broadly. "I'm game if you are."

Within a few minutes, they picked up a saw from Ian's house, picked up Ella from school, and headed up the mountain to pick up a free tree.

"Are we really going to cut down a Christmas tree?" Ella's face shone with excitement, replacing the despondency that sometimes resided there.

Ian peered at her through the rearview mirror, obviously delighted with his daughter's current frame of mind. "Yep."

Ella let out a shriek of excitement, then started chattering on and on about things going on at school. Half an hour later they reached the ski basin and began their trek to a grove of small evergreens that Ian said were the ones the owners wanted cleared. In less than a few minutes, Ella picked one out and Ian cut it down. Next Holly chose the one she wanted. Ian sawed the tree for several minutes, then let Holly take the last few cuts while he took pictures.

Then they quickly loaded up the trees and headed down the hill. Holly breathed a sigh of relief. Was she the only one who had felt some angst that their earlier mountain experience would repeat itself?

The descent into Evergreen was even more spectacular than usual. Not only was it an expansive view, but the sunset was an explosion of red, orange, and yellow. Even Ella stopped her endless chatter as they took in the beautiful sight. Holly released a sigh. If only she could find a way to help Ian believe in the One who made the sunsets. She spent the rest of their time together praying for just such an opportunity.

The sun had just finished setting when they pulled into her driveway. Though the tree was fairly large, in order to fit the scale of the house's great room with its high ceilings, Ian carried it with ease. "Where do you want it?"

She pointed to front windows. "Right over there."

He leaned the tree against a wall near the windows. "Do you have a tree stand?"

Holly shrugged. "There might be one in the stack of Christmas decorations Annie and John have in the garage, but I'm not sure. If there's not one, I'll go buy it."

Ian nodded. "Okay. If you want some help setting this up, just let me know. But for right now, we need a bucket of water for the tree. The fireman inside me has to remind you that you'll need to water it everyday. Don't forget."

"I won't. Thanks for helping me get the tree, and let me know if I can return the favor some way."

His eyes took on a curious light, but he didn't elaborate. Instead he turned and headed to the front door, stepped out of it, and closed it behind him.

Eight

I an climbed into the driver's seat of the Subaru, his heart heavy. He'd been so hopeful that he and Holly would be able to regain some footing today, but obviously that hadn't happened. Though she was communicating with him, it was still all business on her end. He inserted the key into the ignition and buckled his seat belt. While he wasn't eager to rush into anything, he couldn't deny that there was something indefinable between them. Yes, it might be just mutual respect, but it could also potentially be much more.

"Dad, are you okay?"

Ella. He'd even forgotten she was in the back seat. "Yeah, sweetie, I am." He turned in his seat to see her.

Her lips were skewed to one side and her eyes, narrowed. She clearly didn't believe him.

His cell phone started chiming out a familiar tune. That would be Miranda. He put the call on speaker phone. "Hello?"

"Hey, cuz." Her voice sounded a little too chipper for his liking, and he braced himself for what was coming next. "Have you forgotten that tonight is the community tree-lighting?"

"Oh, Dad, can we go? Please?" Ella dragged the last word out into multiple syllables.

He shot Ella a 'get-quiet' look so he could continue the conversation. "Uh, I actually had forgotten, so thanks for the reminder."

"So you're going?" His cousin's tone held a mixture of surprise and excitement. What did she have up her sleeve this time?

Ian peered at Ella with a smile. Just seeing her excitement over cutting down a Christmas tree had shown him that he needed to add at least a little holiday festivity into their lives. "Yeah, we are." Ella started a buckled-up rendition of the happy dance in the back seat.

"Oh, good, because there's someone I've been wanting you to meet."

He pressed his lips together. Just as he'd suspected. "We'll see. Listen, I've got to go. Talk to you later." Without waiting for more, he ended the call just as he pulled up to their house.

Ella insisted on taking the tree in right that minute, spouting off exactly where she thought it should go.

He couldn't help but release a sigh as he pulled the tree from its resting place atop the Subaru. If it weren't for his daughter, he'd be a regular old Scrooge. Why did Christmas have to be so complicated? A few minutes later, he had the tree in the house and went in search of the Christmas tree stand. That way they could get the tree in water and in an upright position in Ella's perfect spot. Once more his mind returned to the situation with Holly, along with Miranda's dogged attempts to set him up with someone. Somehow he had to find a solution to both problems.

Hmm. The wheels began to turn as he pulled out several boxes marked Christmas. By the time he had all the boxes inside, his plan was in place. Then, as if on cue, his phone buzzed. He glanced at the screen. Holly? Calling him? "Hey!"

"Hey, yourself." Amusement resonated in her words. "Listen, I was just looking at the calendar to find a time to meet with you and Holly. Would tomorrow afternoon work?"

"Sorry, but it won't. I have to work."

"What about the next day?"

He checked the fridge calendar. "Sorry. Ella has a program at school." Yet another event that he'd need to keep Miranda's hands out of.

"Goodness, I wasn't counting on how busy you are."

"Especially this time of year." Time to segue into his plan. "But I think I might have an idea that will work for both of us."

"Okay. Let's hear it."

"Earlier you mentioned that if there was ever anything you could do to return the favor. Uh, there is actually one little thing you can do that would help me out a lot."

"Helping people out. That's what I live for."

He couldn't help but laugh.

"Come on. The suspense is killing me. What is this one little thing that will help you out a lot?"

"Tonight is the town-wide Christmas party and tree-lighting ceremony. I have a cousin who is constantly trying to set me up with one of her friends."

"Ah, you have one of those people in your life, too."

Good. At least she could relate to his predicament. "And honestly, the lighting ceremony is just the start of a lot more yet to come." He took a quick breath to gather his courage. "What would you say to coming with us to these events to keep my cousin at bay? That would give us the opportunity to talk. And if you needed to meet with Ella one afternoon while I'm at work, that could be arranged."

Her heavy sigh sounded through the phone. "I get where you're coming from, but I just don't know."

"Please, Holly. I promise to keep it professional and all about business, if that helps."

The other end went silent, which proved two things. First, she was still struggling with the idea of something between them for whatever reason, and second, at least she was considering it. "Please say yes."

"I can't believe I'm saying this, but okay. I'm actually pretty good at warding off people who feel the need to control the lives of others."

"I figured as much. That's why I thought I'd ask. Pick you up around 7:30?"

"Sounds good. See you then. Bye." Her voice held absolutely no smidgen of excitement.

His own excitement waned a bit. Well, at least their arrangement would keep Miranda off his back.

Holly chunked her phone onto the couch and then plopped down beside it, puzzling over the wide range of emotions and thoughts that coursed throughout her. What was she thinking when she said yes to Ian's plan? Not only had she committed herself for tonight, but for who knew how many other events in the future.

She squared her shoulders. Well, she would just have to stick to her guns and keep her heart under lock and key, if not for herself, then for Ella's sake.

Seven-thirty arrived much too quickly, but she had her questions for Ian printed out and folded in her pocket. Who knew? Maybe he'd be so put off by the personal questions that his cousin's option would sound like a better deal.

The doorbell rang.

That would be Ian. She donned her winter gear and then answered the door.

Ian stood there, a tight smile on his face. "Ready?'

"Sure." She pulled the door shut behind her and followed Ian to the Subaru, where he helped her into the vehicle. "Hope I'm dressed okay. I didn't think to ask."

"And I didn't think to tell you." Ian shut the door, moved to the driver's side and climbed in, then backed the car out of the driveway. "You look fine." He didn't even glance her way.

Though his business-only promise was standing true, it also stung a bit. Holly turned to the back seat to where Ella sat. "Hey, girlfriend. Are you ready for the tree-lighting ceremony?"

"What I'm really looking forward to is seeing my friends. Last year the rest of it was pretty lame."

Holly exchanged a glance with Ian. "Well, you neglected to tell me that important piece of information. Had I known it was lame, I probably would have declined your invitation."

Both he and Ella laughed.

Within a few blocks, Holly's eyes widened in awe. "Wow! This doesn't look lame to me at all." There were trees and decorations everywhere, and one gigantic tree stood in the town square, so tall that from the car window she couldn't see the top. And there were people everywhere, talking, laughing, milling about, like something straight from a Hallmark Christmas movie.

"Daddy, there's Stephanie. Can I hang out with her while we're here?"

Ian smiled at her through the rearview mirror. "Sure. We'll meet up at the tree lighting." He pulled into a vacant parking space and removed his wallet from his hip pocket. "Here's some spending money."

She grabbed the twenty-dollar bill he held out and was gone in the blink of an eye.

Ian shook his head. "She's growing up way too fast."

"Just enjoy it while it lasts."

"Easier said than done."

"I'm sure, but you can do it if you try."

His head cocked to one side. "Are you always so upbeat?"

"Well, I'm not Pollyanna, as you suggested soon after we met. But I do try to keep a positive focus when I can. To me, it doesn't seem wise to do anything less."

"You really are like that, aren't you?"

She shrugged. "I am what I am. But I can see how people who don't really know me might see it as phony baloney."

He put a hand over his chest as though mortally wounded. "I'm not sure I phrased it that way."

"No, but it was implied. Don't let it bother you. We all have our faults." She made sure to send a teasing smile to accompany her words, so that he didn't take them more seriously than she meant them.

"Ready to join the fun?"

She looked out the front car window and raised her eyebrows. "Sure. But just as a reminder, we do need to find a place to talk. That's why I agreed to this little plan of yours."

His face took on a wry expression as he opened his door and climbed from the vehicle. "Slave driver."

She didn't respond, mainly because she wanted him to know that she meant business, but also because stepping out of the car door once more reminded her of stepping into a giant, real-life snow globe. And as if on cue, large fluffy snowflakes joined the other beauty around her. Magical! While New York City was beautiful at the holidays, it was more of a tinsel-glistening hustle and bustle kind of beauty.

This, on the other hand, was slower-paced and relaxing, that family-feel that drew her in every time, like a hungry dog to a bone.

"Your face." Ian stood there smiling at her.

"Do I have food somewhere?"

"No, not at all. But just for a minute, your face looked like, well, an angel. If you don't mind me asking, what were you thinking about?"

"How this place is like being in a giant snow globe." Once more the feeling of awe and wonder descended.

Ian smiled, but didn't offer further comment. Instead he showed her around town and enlisted her help in buying some gifts in a few stores. Holly found gifts for both Ian and Darcy. For Darcy, she found a beautiful hand-made knit scarf with an interesting pattern. Under the circumstances, she had almost not purchased a gift for Ian. But when she'd seen the ornament with two skiers on a slope, she couldn't resist. Maybe it would remind him of the day he almost killed her. But the best part was shopping for Ella. She thought back to when she was that age, and tried to think of gift ideas that way. In the end, she relied on Ian to give her a few hints, and settled on a wooden artist's easel, some paints and pastels, and a pad of art paper.

"She'll love that, Holly. But you didn't have to buy all of it. One gift would have been enough."

"I actually loved doing it. There's something special about seeing Christmas through the eyes of a child, you know?"

He nodded, but didn't respond. Based on the faraway look in his eyes, he was remembering times past. She sighed. Though those memories sometimes hurt, it was good to remember the past to hopefully get back to where you needed to be. Maybe this was a good time to find a place to talk.

Ian beat her to a conversation of his choosing. "So. How does this compare to your New York City Christmas parties?"

She thought for a minute. "City parties are more hustle and bustle, more fancy, and..." She nibbled on yet another Christmas cookie. "...um, more gluten-free."

His laughter joined the rest of the sounds of the evening, and melted yet another part of the ice wall around her heart. Okay, it was definitely time for the business end of things. She pointed to a nearby table off to one side. "Ready to talk?"

"Sure, but not there. I have a better idea. Follow me."

She did as he said, but when they finally arrived at his destination, she almost choked. A lovely Christmas red sleigh, complete with black horses decked out in jingle bells stood in front of them. Her heart moved to her throat. Every woman, including herself, had romantic notions tied to sleigh rides in the snow. Just how was she supposed to keep things all business while taking a ride through a winter wonderland?

Once they were situated in the sleigh and had taken off for a moonlight ride around the small lake in the center of town, Ian turned to Holly. "Okay, what did you want to talk about?"

She reached in her coat pocket, pulled out a folded sheet of paper, and used her cell phone as a flashlight.

His mouth went dry. A whole list of questions?

"First, I want to remind you that my goal isn't to get too personal or be nosy. I'm searching for clues that will help me give you and Ella the help you need."

"Okay." How he hated that his voice trembled a bit.

"I don't mean to pry or hurt you, but what was Amy like?"

His heart cracked a bit at just the mention of her name. "Sweet. Kind. Funny. A wonderful mom. She had this way of handling Ella when she got out of hand that just amazed me. She wasn't unnecessarily harsh or one to hand out guilt trips, but she just always knew the right thing to say. And when I got discouraged or frustrated, she could lift my spirits or calm me down with just a glance." He grew silent, his heartache increasing. "There's not a day that goes by that I don't miss her. Especially this time of year."

"Why this time of year?"

"Christmas was her favorite holiday. She wore herself out every year with everything she did to make it special for me and Ella."

"So if it's hard for you at Christmas, don't you think it's also difficult for Ella?"

He nodded. "Yeah, I'm sure that's true. And I'll admit that sometimes I'm so caught up in my own pain during this time of year that I forget to see how Ella's doing. And I have a tendency to make myself overly busy and avoid anything I can that reminds me of her, just to hopefully numb the pain."

"Don't beat yourself up over that, Ian. It happens, and I get that on a personal level."

He turned to face her. "That's right. Your fiancé broke up with you around this time, right?"

She nodded, but immediately launched into her next question. "This may seem like an odd question, but do you believe in God?"

He paused. What was her reason for asking? Was she another one of those people who thought it was her job to save him? Another thought shook him to the core. Would his answer ruin his chance at getting to know her better? He took a deep breath. Never had he met someone so discerning and wise. It would do no good to whitewash the truth with her. "I grew up in church."

"That's not what I asked."

"Okay. Fair enough. To answer your question, at one time I thought I did. But then I changed my mind about all that religious stuff."

"Because of Amy's death?"

"Actually before that, though her death definitely solidified in my mind that God wasn't real. And if he does exist, he obviously isn't the loving God He claims to be."

"What makes you say that?"

"A loving God wouldn't take away a little girl's mother. Don't you agree?"

"No."

"I don't get it. How can you believe He's loving when stuff like that happens? Or maybe it hasn't happened to you. Yet." He pointed a finger her way as his voice and his pulse rocketed upward. "That's why you shouldn't be so upbeat about everything. Life has a way of stepping in to knock those rose-colored glasses off your face."

She grew very quiet, so much so that Ian almost asked if he'd offended her. But she chimed in first. "Just because I choose to look at the world from a positive slant doesn't mean that I haven't had problems."

"I know. You lost your fiancé."

"I lost a lot more than that."

"Like what?" There was no way her loss could compare to his and Ella's.

She shifted in her seat. "We're not here to talk about me. So you don't believe in God at all anymore?"

Hadn't that already been established? But in a flash, a thought dawned. The night he'd prayed to God in desperation. He'd prayed for help, and help had arrived in the form of Holly. "I just thought of something." His voice held a reverent awe that he didn't plan on. "Not too long ago, before you came to town, Ella was going through a bad spell. I prayed that God would send help." He met her gaze. "I think that you could very well be the answer to that prayer."

Her face took on wonder as she considered his words, and her eyes looked as if she were back in time and miles away. Finally she came back to the present. "That's pretty amazing how He works, huh?"

He shrugged. "Or it could just be coincidence."

"I guess it once more comes down to how you choose to look at the world."

"What do you mean?"

"Well, looking back at my own life over the past few weeks, I can see how He led me here. Don't you think that it's at least a possibility that He has helped carry you through the aftermath of Amy's death?"

"I guess it could be possible, but most of the time it sure didn't feel like it."

"Just because life is hard doesn't mean that God's not there." She looked at him directly. "Did Amy believe?"

He nodded. "She did, and so does Ella."

"Has she been attending church?"

"No."

"Why not?"

He sighed, wishing he didn't have to answer. "She's asked to go in the past, but I said no."

"Why?"

"Guess I didn't want her to believe a lie that she would one day recognize as such. You know, like the tooth fairy and Easter bunny."

"Would you be open to letting her go if it helped her emotionally?"

He thought about it and then nodded to the affirmative. "Yeah. I definitely would." He paused, a question burning a hole in his skull? "What about you? Have you been going to church since you came here?"

"No, but I want to. Going to church can be really scary when you don't know anyone."

His thoughts kicked into overdrive. If nothing else, the plan swirling in his thoughts would give him the opportunity to see how Ella would respond. "Would you mind coming to church with me and Ella this coming Sunday? I think it would help both of us."

"You'd actually go?"

"Yes."

Her head lowered. "I want to for so many reasons, but I don't want people to get the wrong idea." She hesitated, deep in thought. "You know, it will be good for all of us, so the answer is yes." Then without skipping a beat, she checked her sheet of paper and segued right into her next question. "If you don't mind me asking, what were the circumstances behind Amy's death?"

"Ovarian cancer."

Her face paled, and for the first time on the sleigh ride, her expression softened. "I'm so sorry, Ian."

"That makes both of us. Cancer of any kind stinks, you know? But I'm so grateful that we at least had time to say our goodbyes, that her death wasn't a sudden thing."

Holly grew very quiet, her head turned toward the Christmas lights reflecting off the lake. As they passed under a large overhead light, Ian looked at her more closely. Streams of tears rivered down her cheeks.

How he longed to comfort her, to help her through whatever loss his words had triggered, but based on her response to him ever since the snow hike and the promise he'd made, he didn't dare. Baby steps, right?

It was only as the sleigh returned to downtown that she came back from wherever she'd been. "Sorry. Guess I got caught up in the scenery." Her voice held her normal chipper tone, the one she donned when trying to be happy. Yet more proof that she sometimes used it as a cover up. She laughed, a forced and hollow sound. "I don't know about you, but I could use an extra-large hot chocolate with extra marshmallows right now."

Ian helped her down from the sleigh. For someone who usually ate so healthy, her craving was yet another clue that she was under stress. "Okay. I know just the place."

As they made their way toward the village shop with the best hot chocolate in town, a voice sounded from behind them. "Ian?"

He and Holly both turned at the same time.

"Hi, Miranda." He put a hand on Holly's shoulder and brought her forward a bit before moving his hand away.

"Holly, this is my cousin Miranda and her husband Dave. And this," he smiled at Holly, "is Holly."

"Nice to meet you, Holly." Miranda's face held a broad, overly-friendly smile. She reached out and shook Holly's hand. "So how do you two know each other?"

"Uh, we're.." Fumbling for words, Holly looked at Ian with a bit of panic in her eyes.

He grabbed her hand and put it through his arm, resting his opposite hand on hers. "We're just good friends." Then just as quickly as he could, he changed the subject. "Well, we'll see you around. Have a good time." With that, he ushered Holly around Miranda and Dave, and on down the street to the hot chocolate Holly had requested. It was only as he reached for his wallet to pay for their drinks that he noticed.

Holly still had her hand tucked in the crook of his arm.

Holly sipped her delicious cup of hot chocolate. All night long she'd struggled to keep her head above water, then with one brief answer, Ian had unintentionally sent her spiraling straight into the blues of missing her parents. She'd been so out of it, she had no idea that she'd kept her arm locked in his while they strolled the streets of downtown Evergreen.

She gave her head a shake in an attempt to change the direction of her thoughts. Well, at least things had gone in the right direction concerning spiritual matters. She thought back to her morning prayer time, when she'd specifically asked the Lord to open doors. He had faithfully delivered, not only in being able to talk openly and honestly about faith, but also in their plans to attend church together this coming Sunday. And Ian was the one who suggested it! She breathed out a silent prayer of praise and thanksgiving to God.

"There you two are!" Ella stood directly in front of them, along with most of the townspeople, right in front of the thirty-foot town tree. "They're about to start the countdown!"

As if on cue, the person at the microphone started counting backwards from ten, and the rest of the crowd joined in. As they reached the number one, the tree lit up, easily rivaling anything she'd ever witnessed in New York City. The difference here was the palpable sense of family, community, and belonging.

"Dad, can we stay a while longer so we can ice skate?"

He checked his watch. "Only for another thirty minutes. Then we need to get you home and in bed. Tomorrow's a school day, you know."

Ella immediately latched on to Holly's hand. "Will you skate with me, Holly?"

"I'd love to, sweetheart. But you probably should know that I'm not that great at ice-skating." The feel of Ella's hand in hers sent the same familiar pain shooting into her heart. And oh, how she already loved Ella's sweet, happy face. *Lord, help me out here. How am I ever going to be able to leave this place?* No, make that these people?

"Maybe. But you can learn, just like you learned to ski." Holly couldn't help but sneak a peek at Ian. Earlier in the week she'd managed her first big girl slope. It hadn't gone perfectly, but she'd made great progress.

Within a few minutes, the three sat on a bench near the ice rink, lacing their rented ice skates. Holly glanced around. Evergreens bedecked with twinkling lights surrounded the rink, and laughter and music tinted the air with pure joy.

Ian helped her stand. "How do you feel?"

"Like a walrus on ice skates. No, make that a giraffe."

He and Ella both laughed. Then, like a skating pro, Ella skated around Holly and latched onto her left hand. "Dad, why don't you go find something else to do? You've been hogging Holly all evening. Now it's my turn."

The girl's sweet words were yet another dagger of bittersweet joy to Holly's heart.

Ian feigned a hurt look. "Fine. Be that way." He followed his words with a wink before he skated off, making ice skating look effortless.

Holly looked down at Ella. "Hope you don't mind going at a snail's pace."

"Nope. Have you had a good time?"

"It's been wonderful."

"What all did you do?"

"Well, we went shopping, ate some cookies, drank some hot chocolate, ate some more cookies..."

Ella giggled, then she grew serious. "I saw you getting into the sleigh."

"Yes, your dad took me on a sleigh ride around the lake."

"He and mom and I used to do that every year." Her voice was laced with sorrow.

"I'm sorry, sweetie. I didn't know."

Ella shrugged. "I know. I just miss her so badly."

Holly sighed. Was she emotionally in a place where she could help Ella through this? Just one look at the girl's face gave her the answer she sought. "The holidays seem to be some of the hardest days to get through when we lose someone we love."

Ella cocked her head to one side. "Have you ever lost someone you loved?"

The question knocked the wind from her lungs.

"You don't have to answer, Holly." Ella's eyes searched her face. "I think I already know the answer anyway."

Holly racked her brain for something to say that would turn the conversation around. "Your dad told me that your mother loved Christmas and always made it very special for you."

A soft smile turned up the corners of the little girl's mouth. "She did. That's one reason I love Christmas so much. But it's also why it's so hard. Why does it work that way?"

Great question. "I don't know, but it certainly does work that way."

Ella grew quiet, her thoughts obviously on the past and her mom. Then without warning, she asked another question that sent Holly reeling, not just her thoughts, but her skates as well. "Are you falling in love with my dad?'

The next thing she knew, Holly was on her backside staring up at the starlit night. In the next instant, Ian was right beside her, down on all fours, his face full of concern. "Are you okay?"

This was turning into a bizarre pattern. First the ski lesson, then the bunny slope, and now this. "I...I think so."

"I'm really sorry, Holly." The words came from Ella, who stood nearby.

"It's okay, sweetie. It wasn't your fault."

"Feel like sitting up?" Ian's face came back into focus.

"Yeah, at least, I think so."

He sat down on the ice next to her and put an arm under her neck and shoulders, gently lifting her upward.

But no sooner had she made it to a sitting position, her head began to spin. "Whoa. I'm so dizzy."

Ian gently laid her head against his arm, so that her face was only inches from his. The look on his face carried the same agony she felt, like she was drowning and incapable of coming up for air. For what seemed like an eternity, there was only Ian and herself. Everything else faded into the background.

Then Holly somehow found the strength to force her eyes away. The first face she saw was Ella's. The girl had witnessed it all, and she knew. It was written all over her face.

Ella turned quickly and skated away.

Nine

After making sure that Holly would be fine without anyone to watch after her, Ian and Ella made their way back out to the Subaru. Somewhat put out at Ella's rude behavior inside, Ian did all he could to curb his frustration and talk some sense into his daughter. "Mind me asking why you turned so sour all of a sudden?"

She didn't answer as they climbed into the car and pulled out of the driveway, but finally she spoke. "You almost kissed her."

"No I didn't."

"Yes you did. I was standing right there, Dad, so don't pretend it didn't happen."

Ian pulled onto their road, all the while searching his heart. It was true, and he'd tried to deny it. But how could he explain to ten-year-old what he couldn't even explain to himself? "I'm sorry, Ella. I guess maybe we did almost kiss. I don't know why, but I am sorry that it upset you." He pulled into the garage, put the car in park, and waited for a response from her, but none came. "And I'm sorry you saw the whole thing. I'm sure that was awkward and uncomfortable for you."

A sniffle sounded from the backseat. "You took her on a sleigh ride around the lake."

Was there anything she hadn't seen? "Yes."

"Why didn't you invite me?"

Oh, so that was the instigating event. "There were some things we needed to talk about privately."

The sniffles turned to sobs.

"Ella, sweetheart, please don't cry."

Now her sobs turned to angry words. "You're falling in love with her, aren't you? And she's falling in love with you. What about Mom, huh? Are you forgetting all about her?"

"No, Ella. I could never forget about your Mom."

She started crying again. "If Mom had been here, I would have been invited to ride the sleigh around the lake."

The words knifed into him. She was right. It was something they always did together every year. Yet another family Christmas tradition. No wonder Ella was so angry. "I'm really sorry about everything, Ella. I didn't mean to exclude you. I just wasn't thinking. Please forgive me."

The sobs continued.

How could he help her understand? Would now be a good time to tell her that he'd hired Holly to help them both get past this impasse that seemed to grow larger than the Rockies by the second?

Her cries continued, shredding his heart.

He had to try something, anything to get her to stop crying. "The reason Holly and I were talking is because I've hired her to help both of us get through this, this whatever-it-is that we can't seem to get past."

It worked. She stopped crying. "You hired her? Without asking me about it first? And what is she? Some kind of doctor?"

Maybe the crying was better than the belligerent anger. "She has degrees in psychology, and she's a well-respected health and wellness coach."

"That doesn't sound helpful at all."

"I felt the same at first, Ella, but I researched her online. She's here, and she wanted to help us. That's what makes her heart happy--helping people. It was either that or drive to the city on a regular basis. I didn't think either one of us wanted that or could manage it with our schedules."

The backseat grew quiet. That was a good sign, right?

She finally spoke, her voice soft and controlled. Almost too controlled. "How long?"

"How long what?"

"How long ago did you hire her?"

He swallowed, wishing that he didn't have to tell her. Because he was pretty sure she wasn't going to like it. "Last week."

In a flash, Ella unbuckled and catapulted herself from the backseat, running into the house and slamming the door behind her.

Ian cut off the Subaru and followed her into the house. "Ella!"

Down the hall, her bedroom door slammed.

He hurried to the door and tried the door knob. Locked. "Ella, unlock this door right this minute."

Loud sobs resumed, once more tearing at his heart.

He looked up at the ceiling and raked a hand through his hair, sucking in big gulps of air. "Ella, please let me in so we can talk."

Her sobs subsided a bit, but her words were interspersed with cries and sniffles. "I can't right now, Dad. I just need to think through everything first, okay?"

That was a first. Maybe she was making progress. "Okay. Do you have any questions I can answer?"

Silence shrouded their tiny cabin, but finally she spoke. "Only one."

He smiled in relief. More progress. "What's that, honey?"

"So every time I saw Holly, she was just being nice to me because you hired her? 'Cause that's what it feels like to me."

"What do you mean by you almost kissed him?" Darcy's voice sounded a bit panicked, even through the phone.

Holly scrambled for words to explain something that was totally unexplainable. "I--I don't know. It was just one of those weird things. I really think that I almost kissed him. And Ella saw the whole thing." Her words came out as a semi-wail.

"Okay, that's it. I'm taking some vacation time and coming down to see you."

"That's totally unnecessary, Darcy."

"Maybe to you, but I need to check this guy out. If you ask me, he sure seems to be coming on strong in a very short amount of time."

Holly shook her head, only accentuating the ache from last night's spill on the ice. "Then I've obviously painted the wrong picture. It's me. What's wrong with me? He and his daughter are my clients, for heaven's sake."

"I'm hanging up now to make my reservations. I'll call you back later."

Holly started to object, but the line went dead. She laid her phone on the coffee table and gently laid her throbbing head back against the couch. Great. Just great. Why did everything have to be so complicated?

Her phone jingled. She answered it. "Well that didn't take long."

"I tried to call sooner, but it went straight to your voice mail."

Ian. "Oh, sorry. I thought you were someone else."

He laughed. "I gathered as much. Thought I'd call and see how you're feeling today."

"Like someone slapped me upside the face with a wrecking ball."

"That bad, huh? Can I do anything for you? Do you need to see a doctor?"

She resisted the urge to tell him that he'd done more than enough. "No thanks, but I probably won't make it to ski lessons this afternoon." At least her massive headache gave her a good excuse.

"Because of your head, or something else?"

Her mouth went dry. How was she supposed to answer that? "I...uh...yeah, my head."

The other end went completely quiet.

"Are you still there?"

"Yeah, I'm here." She could almost picture the look on his face by the tone of his voice. "You know, Holly, at some point we're going to have to stop tiptoeing around this issue and bring it out in the open."

"There's nothing to bring out in the open. I'm not going to let that happen."

He laughed, but not out of amusement. Instead the sound had a sharp curt edge to it. "There you go again, trying to control things. Let me guess. Not part of your life plan?" His words were edged with hurt.

"It's not that, Ian. If circumstances were different--"

"No, you mean if circumstances were perfect. We've talked about this before. That's just not how life works, and sooner or later we will have to face this like grown-ups."

She struggled to find words, but whether because of her throbbing head or some other reason, she just couldn't answer.

His heavy sigh sounded through the phone. "I have a favor to ask."

"Okay."

There's a night ski session on Thursday night, and a friend of mine has a conflict and asked me to cover his shift. I can pick Holly up from school, but I need someone to keep her until I can get home. You two seem to be hitting it off, and I thought it might help you have more opportunity for conversation."

"Yeah, of course, I'd be happy to."

"I really appreciate it, and I know Ella will be excited. Hope your head feels better soon."

"Thanks. Bye." She huffed out a huge sigh. The conversation hadn't gone great, but it could have been far worse.

A few minutes after that, Darcy called again. "I fly into Denver on Saturday morning. The plane lands at six a.m. Can you pick me up?"

"Sure." Only later, after she and Darcy had said their goodbyes, did she realize the benefit of having Darcy here. Her friend would serve as a buffer at a time when she sorely needed one. Darcy would also be able to go to church with her, Ian, and Ella on Sunday, an added bonus to be sure.

Then a sudden thought dawned. With this massive headache was it safe for her to drive? And even without the headache, would she be able to maneuver the mountainous drive and Denver traffic in the dark to pick up Darcy?

Thursday afternoon the doorbell rang, and Holly wiped her hands on a kitchen towel and headed to the door.

Ian stood there, next to a very sullen Ella. "We're here!" Then he gestured and mouthed the words. "She's having a bad day."

Holly squatted down on eye-level with Ella. "Man, am I glad you're here today. I was just about to spruce up this place for the holidays, and I could really use an extra pair of hands. Do you like baking Christmas cookies?"

Ella's head drooped, but Ian did an amazing job of not rushing to her rescue like he usually did. A few seconds later, she raised her head. "I guess that sounds okay. Mom and I used to make Christmas cookies together." She sent a pointed glare Ian's way.

Holly frowned, but quickly replaced it with her chipper tone. "Well, it's good to know that I have experienced help." She stood back up, facing Ian. "You don't have to worry about her. We're going to have a lot of fun, aren't we, Ella?"

Ella shrugged. "I guess."

Ian smiled at both of them, but ended by making eye contact with Holly. "I know she's in good hands." He looked at Ella. "Be nice for Holly, okay?"

The girl didn't respond.

Ian sent Holly an apologetic grin. "Well, guess I'd better be going."

"Before you leave, can I ask you a favor?"

His eyebrows shot upward.

She smiled. "It's my turn."

He returned the smile, a humorous glint in his eyes. "That it is. What do you need?"

"My best friend Darcy is flying into Denver early Saturday morning. Her plane lands at six. Would you mind taking me? I normally wouldn't ask, but I'm not sure I could find my way there in the dark."

"I don't mind at all." He checked his watch. "But we'll have to hash out the details later."

"Sounds good."

After he left for work, Holly led Ella back to the kitchen. "Ready to get started?"

Though the girl didn't smile or respond, she jumped right into the cookie-making process.

Holly kept trying to draw her into conversation, but without any luck. The lighting ceremony. Was she still upset about that? Holly allowed her thoughts back to turn to the events of that night. Ella had been totally silent afterwards. Well, no matter the reason, it was obviously time to quit tiptoeing around and cut straight to the point. "Ella, I think you're mad at me about something. Would you please tell me why so that we can talk about it?"

"You sound just like my dad." She sighed. "I know why you've been so nice to me."

Holly frowned. "What are you talking about?"

"Dad told me that he hired you to help us."

Holly quit stirring the bowl of cookie dough and went to stand right in front of Ella. "Sweetie, I'm not just being nice to you because of that. I hope you know that. I truly care about you, and I want to help. That's what I do for lots of people."

Ella didn't look like she bought a word that Holly spoke. Her eyes narrowed. "You never answered my question from the other night."

"What question?"

"Are you falling in love with my dad?"

Just as she'd suspected. They'd finally arrived at the true heart of the problem. "I don't know how to answer that, Ella. It's not what I want to happen. In fact, I've done everything I know to keep that from happening." She sat down on the bar stool next to Ella. "I think part of what I'm experiencing has to do with the time of the year, sort of like we talked about the other night. Do you know what I mean?"

"You mean about the holidays being hard."

"Yes." Should she say more?

"Are you lonely?"

The question took Holly by surprise. "Yeah, I guess I am. I came here to hopefully escape the holiday blues, but I don't know anyone except you and Ian."

Ella studied her face, then sent a sad little smile. "Thank you for being honest with me, Holly."

"Can I ask you a question now?"

"Sure."

"Why does all this bother you so much?"

Ella's dark eyes widened as she thought through the question. "Wow, you are good at this. I hadn't even stopped to ask why I was so upset about everything. I think it bothers me because not only does it feel like we're not being fair to mom, but because I'm afraid Daddy won't care about me anymore."

"Well, first off, I know that your Daddy loves you very much. And if you think about it long enough, I think you know that as well." She didn't break eye contact with Ella or try to force her to answer. Instead she just waited.

Ella finally nodded her head. "Yeah, you're right. He would never stop loving me."

"Smart girl. It's important to remember that not every thought that pops into our heads is the truth. Sometimes it's a lie. And it's important to learn how to recognize those lies so that you can overcome them with the truth."

Ella nodded. "That makes a lot of sense. So you're saying to take time to think about whether my thoughts are true or not before I react."

"Exactly. Now let's talk about the first part of what you said, the part about being unfair to your mother. Would your mom want you and your Dad to be happy?"

Ella nodded. "Yeah, she would."

"So if your Dad found someone else--especially someone you cared about and who cared about you--don't you think your Mom would want that to happen?"

She nodded again, but her eyes still held sorrow. "In my head, I know that she would want that. But it just is hard for my heart to know it too."

Now Holly smiled. "Very well said. It's always easier to accept things with our mind than it is with our heart.

And for me, problems always pop up when my head and heart can't agree."

"Can your head and heart agree about how you feel about Daddy?"

Holly gave her head a sad little shake. Leave it to a child to pinpoint the problem. Her heart wanted to let go, to enjoy the roller coaster ride that Ian had mentioned. But her head. There was no way she could or would allow her head to go there. "Ella, my life is in New York City, just like yours is here in Evergreen. Besides that, your dad asked me to help him and you. If I allow myself to get involved with the two of you past the point of trying to help you, it just feels wrong. I don't want to let that happen because I'll be leaving in a few weeks. I don't want to hurt you or your dad."

"But aren't you doing your work from here now? I mean, you could technically still work from Evergreen, right?"

"Yes, I could." Though it killed her to have to admit it.

"But...?"

Holly's anguished heart released the answer she'd been seeking for days. "But what if it doesn't work out? Then there's three hurting people who are even more hurt. I don't want that for any of us."

"But if it does work out, then you've turned three sad people into three happy people."

Holly sputtered, trying to find words, but in the end, gave up in defeat. "You put me to shame, girlfriend. I'm supposed to be the one who puts an upbeat and positive spin on everything, and you just beat me at my own game."

Ella laughed out loud, truly smiling for the first time that day, but then, just as quickly, she sobered. "So that leaves us back where we started. How do we know what to do?"

Holly's thoughts instantly turned to the verses that had latched hooks in her heart. "Our job is never to figure things out, even though I often spend days trying to do just that."

"We're not supposed to try and figure things out?"

"This might be hard for you to understand, but your dad mentioned that you believe in God."

Ella nodded.

"When we belong to Him, we don't have to figure it all out. All we have to do is--"

"--trust Him." Ella spoke the words with hushed awe. "Mama used to say the same thing." Then she sighed. "But that's not as easy as it sounds."

"It's sure not. I promise myself that I'm not going to worry or try to figure things out, that all I'm going to do is trust God and live in a way that I think would please Him. And usually within a few minutes' time, I'm already back at it, worrying over things beyond my control and trying to figure things out."

Ella cocked her head to one side. "I just thought of something that I hadn't thought of before."

Holly made her way back to the bowl of cookie dough and started rolling it into balls and dropping it on the cookie sheet. "What's that?"

"Trying to figure things out is what we do with our head. Trusting God is something we do with our heart."

Holly once more stopped her work and shared a smile with the wisest ten-year old she'd ever met. She half-laughed, her eyes brimming with tears, and shook her head from side to side.

"I did it again, didn't I?" asked Ella.

"Did what?"

"Showed you up."

Both of them burst into laughter. From that time forward, the air was clear between them. They spent the rest of their time in the kitchen laughing and talking and eating just as many cookies as those left on the plate.

After the cookies were baked and decorated, Ella looked at Holly very pointedly. "The next thing we need to do is get your tree decorated. It looks so...so..."

"Naked?"

Ella laughed. "Exactly."

Holly pointed to some boxes sitting beside the tree. "I talked to Annie the other day, and she told me where to find their decorations."

Soon the two were busy hanging decorations, chatting, and even singing Christmas songs.

Ella giggled. "Today reminds me of that song."

"Which song?"

"It's beginning to look a lot like Christmas," Ella sang out the words. "We learned it at school. I'm just so glad to be able to decorate a tree."

"Haven't you and your Dad decorated yours?"

Ella lowered her gaze and shook her head from side to side. "No. It's in the stand, but Dad keeps making excuses. We didn't decorate last year either. When Mom was alive we decorated every year. Dad even used to dress up like Santa Claus and bring me presents. But not since Mom died. It's almost like Christmas died when she did." Without warning, her big eyes flooded with tears. "Daddy even took down all the pictures of Mama."

With her heart in her throat, Holly stooped and hugged Ella. "I'm sure it's only because your Dad was afraid it would remind you of your mom."

"I think so too. But I want to remember her. I don't want to forget."

Later that night, after dinner, after the tree and the house had been decorated from top to bottom, Holly found *It's a Wonderful Life* on television for the two of them to watch together. But close to the end of the movie, Holly looked over at Ella to find her sound asleep, a contented smile at rest on her sweet face.

When Ian showed up a few minutes later, Holly signaled for him to be quiet by holding a finger to her lips. "Ella's asleep."

He pulled off his toboggan and peered around the space. "Wow. You guys have been busy."

Holly nodded, a smile curving her lips. "It's been a great day."

A soft laugh sounded as his eyes landed on the Christmas tree.

"I think it's the prettiest tree I've ever had," said Holly. "When I was a little girl my Dad accused me of intentionally trying to pick out the scrawniest tree on the lot just so it would have a home."

"Sounds just like you." The kind smile in his eyes let her know that he found the comment both telling and touching. Finally he broke away from her gaze and cleared his throat. "I see that Ella still has a tendency to load the bottom of the tree with ornaments."

She smiled. "Yes, but it's not about what the decorations look like. It's about enjoying time together." Would her hint work?

His smile faded and a tiny frown drew his eyebrows together. He lowered his head momentarily and then moved to the living room. Ian stared down at his little girl, his eyes full of love. "She looks so happy."

"I think doing Christmas things--things she would have done with her mom--really helped."

Her words seemed to pain him, and a wide range of emotions flashed across his face. He once more lowered his head to stare at his toboggan for a long minute. "I guess I thought that it would be too painful for her. Bring back too many memories. Guess it was just another way I was trying to come to her rescue."

"Is that why you took down all the pictures of your wife?"

His lips flat-lined. "Ella told you?"

Holly nodded.

"It was my decision to make."

"That's true, but don't forget that your actions also affect others."

Without responding, Ian moved to the couch and lifted a sleeping Ella into his arms, setting off an ache in Holly's chest that her deep-breathing exercises would never be able to erase.

Ten

"Holly!" Ian's voice called out behind her Friday afternoon, just as she was getting ready to leave from her first day of solo skiing.

She turned to see him jogging across the ski basin parking lot toward her. "Hey, Ian."

He reached her and smiled down, his dimples making a rare appearance. "Hey. How'd your first day alone go?"

"What's beyond marvelous and fantastic?"

"I can tell. Your face is glowing."

She made a face. "That might be because I forgot to bring sunscreen."

He laughed, but made no comment.

"Is there something you needed?"

"Actually, yes. I hate to even ask, but need to ask you for another favor. If you can't do it, I certainly understand."

"Well, I won't know unless you go ahead and ask."

He grinned. "Um, my parents want to come see me and Ella this year for Christmas, but we just don't have room in our tiny cabin. They offered to get a hotel, but I really would hate that for them on so many levels. Would you mind hosting them at your house? I've already talked to Annie, and she's okay with it."

Relief flooded Holly's entire being. She'd been worried about spending Christmas Day alone for well over a week now. "Not at all. In fact, it will help me out a lot. I really wasn't looking forward to spending Christmas Day all alone." Again.

"Good." His eyes held a knowing gleam of empathy. "Too many memories?"

She nodded, unable to speak because of the knot lodged in her throat. Bruce he knew about, but not her Mom and Dad.

"What can I help you do to get ready for their visit?"

Suddenly a gigantic list loomed in her head. "Oh! Well, I want to put up outdoor lights for sure. And the shopping. And cooking." Now she was regretting volunteering so quickly.

"Don't stress out. Ella and I will help you." He paused, and something about his face suggested that he wanted to say something else.

She turned her head to one side and sent him a questioning gaze. "Yes?"

"I don't know if this is a good idea or not, but I was thinking about maybe bringing over some of our family decorations for your house since we'll be spending our holiday time there." His eyes held uncertainty mixed with fear.

Holly looked up at the blue sky and sent a silent thank you for yet another answered prayer. "I think it's a wonderful idea. Bring them on over. That way my tree won't look so bare on the top half."

A laugh sounded, once more revealing his dimples. "Deal. Do you have plans for later tonight? Ella and I can bring a pan of homemade tamales, and then we can decorate."

"Well, since you put it that way, how can I refuse?"

"Six-thirty?"

"Perfect."

At only three minutes past six-thirty, the doorbell rang. Holly hurried to the front door, eager to see them both.

A blur of fluffy pink coat landed in her arms. "Holly!"

Holly hugged Ella tight and swung her around. She glanced up at Ian's beaming face. "Hey, Ella! I've missed you."

Ella pulled back and stated matter-of-factly, "It's only been one day, you know."

"Really? It felt like at least two weeks." She rose to her feet. "Come on in. I made some guacamole, black beans, Spanish rice, and chicken tortilla soup to go with the tamales, which by the way smell mouth-watering delicious."

Ian closed the door behind him. "Sounds like a feast. Hope you don't expect to have any leftovers." He set the boxes he carried on the counter and handed her the one on top. "Here are the tamales. They might need to be heated a bit more. Where do you want me to put these decorations?"

"By the tree is fine."

Within a few minutes, they all sat around the table.

Focused on the homemade tamales, Holly picked up her fork, ready to dig in. But Ian reached over and put a hand on her arm, drawing her attention to him.

Ian sent an apologetic smile. "Do you mind if I say the blessing first?"

There was nothing she could do to keep her eyebrows in their normal position. Well, this was an interesting development. "Oh, sorry. Please do." She sat her fork on her plate. When she looked up, Ian and Ella were holding hands, and each held out a hand toward her as well. She latched on to both of them, with a reminder to her heart that her time here would soon be over and to keep her head on straight. But one knowing look from Ella also reminded her to just trust God and quit trying to figure everything out.

Ian bowed his head, eyes closed. "God, thank You for everything You are doing." His voice took on a choked sound, and it took a minute for Ian to gain control of his emotions enough to speak. "Thank you for the food and company You've provided. Amen."

Holly's heart overflowed with gratitude. A baby step in the right direction. As she passed the plate of homemade tortillas, she felt Ian's eyes on her, but she just couldn't let him see that her own eyes were brimming with tears right now. How would she ever survive this special time with them, knowing that it was only temporary?

Ella downed her food quickly, then took her dishes to the kitchen. In a split second, she was back at the table.

"Can we decorate now?" Her sweet face held eager excitement.

Ian looked over at Holly. "What do you think? Should we let her get started while we finish our dinner?"

Good. He was truly working on giving her more freedom. "Absolutely." She smiled at Ella. "Earlier today I moved some ornaments around so you'd have more room."

Ella let out a shriek and bounded into the front room where the tree stood. The sounds of boxes opening and the humming of Jingle Bells came from the area.

Ian smiled at her. "Thank you for all this."

"Happy to help. And like I said, it keeps me from dreading Christmas Day." It was only *after* Christmas Day that she dreaded now. The part when she went back to the city and left her heart in Evergreen.

"I don't just mean for hosting my parents and letting us come over on Christmas." He reached over and grabbed her hand. "Even though I'm so very grateful for that." He looked toward the Christmas tree. "But I'm also so grateful for all that you've done for both Ella and me. I totally misjudged you the first time I met you."

She tried to keep a serious face, but just couldn't. "Are you referring to the day you intentionally tried to kill one of your ski students?"

He laughed. "Yeah. That day. Sorry."

"Happy to help in that way, too." She forked a bite of tamale in her mouth, and sent him a smirk. "And I'm especially grateful that your plan to kill me was a total failure."

Now his laugh came out so loud that Ella momentarily hurried in to see what was going on before rushing back to the tree. Ian sent another grateful smile. "I don't know what happened between you and Ella yesterday, but she's a totally different kid today."

Holly looked toward the area where Ella was digging in the box. "She's a very special young lady."

They locked gazes for a long minute. Finally, Holly forced her eyes away from his and rose to her feet. "I'm stuffed, so I'm going to put my dirty dishes in the kitchen and go help Ella." She could feel his questioning eyes on her, but she somehow managed to keep her eyes focused on something other than his handsome face.

After depositing her dishes in the sink, Holly found Ella engrossed in a box of Christmas ornaments. She stood and watched for just a minute.

The sweet girl would carefully pick one up, examine it carefully, and then either hang it on the tree or put it back in the box. Holly puzzled over Ella's process. But why?

Holly moved to the tree as if just entering the room. "Good job, Ella. You already have quite a few on the tree. Way to go!"

Ella beamed at her in a way that totally reminded her of Ian, then moved over to stand beside her. "Look at this one!" She pointed to a popsicle stick reindeer. "I made it in kindergarten." Then she pointed to a construction paper and glitter ornament with a photograph in the center. "And that's me when I was really little."

Holly examined the photo closely. "You were a cute little munchkin even then."

Ella moved to the box and picked out a clear ornament with writing on the side. "But I don't know what this one is."

Ian's voice sounded from the doorway. How long had he been standing there watching them? "Your mama made that for you for your very first Christmas."

Ella frowned. "I won't put it on the tree if it bothers you, Daddy."

Holly's throat cinched tight. So that's why Ella had put some of the decorations back in the box.

Ian's face contorted, and then in a heartbeat, he was kneeling before her. "I want you to do whatever makes you feel good, Ella. You don't have to protect me, sweetheart. We both miss her, but I might have messed up in trying to avoid doing anything that reminded either one of us of her."

Ella threw her hands around his neck. "It's okay, Daddy. I know you were only trying to help. Are you sure you don't mind if I hang it on the tree?"

He pulled back and smiled, his eyes bright with tears. "Not at all. I see it as a celebration of one of the best days in my life. The day you were born. Mind if I help you hang it? I think Gigi and Poppy will be happy to see it as well."

"I know just where to put it." Ella was back to business now, and she pointed to a spot in the front, near the top. "Put it way up there."

When at long last their family decorations were added to the mix, they all stood back to take in the final results.

"It's even prettier than before." Ella whispered the words.

Holly put an arm around the young girl's shoulder. "I agree." It was if the added decorations were meant to go with the look Holly had wanted all along. And she didn't know whether to laugh or cry.

"Ella, I hate to be a party pooper, but we need to get you home and in bed. We've got to get up early in the morning to go pick up Holly's friend at the airport." Ian spoke the words, then began gathering up the boxes.

Instant relief flooded over Holly. She'd loved having them here. Loved helping in whatever way she could. But her emotions were on overload at the moment, and she sorely needed time to sort them all out. And the Lord surely must have known that she really needed Darcy at the minute, even more than she first realized.

She walked the two out to the driveway, and looked on as Ian loaded the boxes in the back and made sure Ella was buckled in.

But rather than get in the car and drive away, he made an intentional trip to where she stood. His eyes searched her face for a long, excruciating moment. "Look, I don't know what's going on in your head right now, but you were different during the past hour than you were at dinner. Are you okay?"

She released a sigh. "I will be, Ian. Please just be patient with me."

"If this is too much--"

"No. I want to do this." Ella needed it. She'd just have to find a way to heal her own broken heart later.

"We'll tackle the outside lights one day next week."

"Okay."

She stood and watched them back out the driveway and head down the road. Though they only lived one house down, just watching them leave created a palpable emptiness and loneliness inside. She sighed and squared her shoulders. Just something else she'd have to learn to live with. She shook her head as she made her way inside. No, make that something else she'd have to learn to live without.

At the Denver airport the next morning, Ian hung back beside Ella to watch Holly greet her friend as she deboarded the plane. He had to admit that he felt more than a little nervous about meeting Holly's best friend, a feeling he wasn't all that accustomed to. If he were to have any chance with Holly, he had to make a positive impact on her friend. That was a well-known unwritten rule. On the trip down, Holly had mentioned that Darcy made the call to visit because she was worried about Holly. Did her worry have anything to do with him?

Holly and Darcy screamed and hugged as though they hadn't seen each other in years, and it was easy to see by the happy smiles and moist eyes that they truly cared for one another.

Holly latched on to her friend's hand and pulled her toward him and Ella. "Come on. I want you to meet my Colorado friends. This living doll is Ella."

Darcy bent low and stuck out her hand, which Ella took in a handshake. "Nice to meet you Ella. Holly was right. You are gorgeous! And I also hear that you are one smart cookie."

Ella blushed, but the smile on her face let everyone know that she was pleased by the compliments.

Holly's features took on a strained edge as she pointed to him. "And this is Ella's dad, Ian."

A smirk landed on Darcy's face as she stepped forward to shake his hand. "Hi, Ian. So you're the guy who almost killed my bestie on the ski slopes."

He took her hand. "Don't believe everything she tells you. If I had really wanted to kill her, I would have succeeded. Nice to meet you, Darcy."

Darcy seemed a bit taken aback. Like she hadn't expected him to come right back at her. She exchanged a knowing look with Holly, but didn't verbally respond.

He glanced down at the large bag she carried. "May I help you with your carry-on?"

Now Darcy's face took on surprise. "Oh. Sure. Thank you so much."

All of them headed to baggage pickup, and within half an hour, had picked up Darcy's luggage and made their way to the parking lot.

"Daddy, I'm hungry. Can we stop and get some breakfast?" Ella's voice held a bit of a whine.

"I was just about to suggest that," joined in Holly. "My treat."

Darcy elbowed Ian. "We'd better take her up on that offer. She doesn't eat out at restaurants often. Only when she wants to celebrate, which is my guess in this case, since I'm here." She gave her long blond hair a dramatic toss, then frowned. "Although she also does it when she's in need of some unhealthy comfort food. Me, on the other hand, I can do unhealthy 24/7."

Ian grinned. He could see why Holly and Darcy were such good friends. They balanced each other out. One was somewhat reserved and a planner. The other spoke whatever was on her mind and probably did everything on impulse, including the trip here. He came to a stop at the Subaru, unlocked it, and loaded Darcy's luggage. "I know just the place. It's not far."

Since it was Saturday, the restaurant that normally filled up early on weekday mornings had plenty of seats when they arrived. As they scanned the menus, Darcy called his name. "Ian, what do you recommend."

"I think everything's tasty, but my personal favorite is huevos rancheros."

"Excuse me?"

"Huevos rancheros."

"Huevos means eggs in Spanish," explained Ella.

"I can do eggs," exclaimed Holly, closing her menu. "That's what I'll have." She smiled at Ian. "At your recommendation, of course."

Darcy sent her an 'oh-puh-lease' look. "Yeah, well, you can eat healthy if you want. I'm going with something to put a little more meat on my bones, like some biscuits and gravy."

Holly grimaced. "Oh, you mean the heart attack on a plate."

In the end, Darcy got her biscuits and gravy while the other three had the huevos rancheros. When the waitress delivered their order, Holly frowned. "What's that green stuff on top?"

"Green chilies." Ella licked her lips. "They're delicious."

"Uh, chilies, as in peppers?"

Ian couldn't help but laugh. "Yep."

"Are they hot?"

"I don't think so, but most people not from the area would disagree."

Darcy nudged her friend. "Don't believe it. He's the guy that tried to kill you, remember?" She eyed Holly's plate. "And forget the green stuff, who would eat eggs on top of those black beans?"

"They're good for you." Ian and Holly spoke in tandem.

Darcy's eyebrows rose. "Well, well, well, you two certainly seem to be on the same page." She paused momentarily, her eyes narrowed and one corner of her mouth on the rise. "At least when it comes to food."

Holly lowered her head without replying, but then dug into her huevos rancheros. Though she did drink a lot of water with the dish, she cleaned her plate, than sat back with a groan, her hands on her belly. "I think that was the best thing I've ever tasted. I just wish I hadn't eaten so much. Or so fast."

He locked eyes with her, while Darcy and Ella chatted away, and rather than quickly looking away, she continued to almost defiantly look his way, an unspoken communication taking place between them. Ian couldn't help but smile, totally enjoying the unexpected moment. This was so not normal behavior for Miss-Plan-Everything."

They both snapped out of it when Darcy cleared her throat. "Sorry to interrupt your little unspoken conversation, but there are at least two of us who feel a little left out."

Now Holly blushed and lowered her head, pretending to dig through her purse.

"Is there a shopping mall nearby?" Darcy directed the question to Ian. "I wanted to get Holly a gift before I left the city, but there just wasn't time."

Before he could respond, Ella chimed in. "That would be awesome, Daddy. That way Holly could help me pick out a gift for you."

Ian looked at Holly, but she kept her gaze averted. "Sounds like a plan. You okay with it, Holly?"

"Uh, sure." She didn't even look his way.

A little later, they entered the mall through one of the department stores. Ella quickly latched on to Holly's arm. "Would you help me, Holly?"

Holly's face lit with a loving smile. "How could I say no to that sweet face? Of course I'll help you." Then she looked at Darcy with a sheepish expression on her face. "I guess that leaves you two to fend for yourselves."

"Perfect." Darcy had a cat-who-ate-the-canary grin on her face, as though things were working out just as she hoped.

Ian's neck muscles tightened. Would he pass the test? He forced himself to relax, choosing to look at the event from a more positive slant. This was the perfect time to learn more about Holly. They all agreed on a meeting place and time, then headed off in different directions.

"Are you looking for anything in particular?" asked Ian.

"I'll know it when I see it. So let's just walk and talk, shall we?"

He nodded. "Of course."

Darcy moved to a rack of women's dresses in a nearby department store. "Just so you know, Holly and I are like sisters. So I think I should be upfront with you from the get-go."

"Okay." He pushed his hands deeper in his pockets, wondering where in the world this conversation was about to go.

"I don't take kindly to people who hurt her." She raised her gaze to him, every pore of her face completely sincere and carved from granite.

"The thing on the ski slope, I--"

"That's not what I'm talking about here. Holly's had it rough, and she has a tender heart. Step lightly, and don't play games."

"I don't intend to."

She returned to looking at the dresses. "That's what they all say."

"All?"

She snorted. "Holly's not the sort to have a string of boyfriends in the wings, Ian. That's not what I meant."

"Then what did you mean?"

"I meant that guys are really good at not intending to hurt anyone, but somehow it always happens."

He nodded. "I see where you're coming from, but that's not who I am."

Darcy locked gazes with him, her eyes searching his face. Hard. Finally she let him go. "I can see that about you."

What was she? Some kind of mind reader or something?

She wandered to another rack nearby and started the same process of shuffling through the dresses one at a time.

Maybe now was a good time to ask a few questions of his own. "Uh...you mentioned that Holly has had a hard life. She told me about her fiancé dumping her at Christmas."

Darcy's features visibly tightened, and her lips clamped together momentarily. "Still makes me mad when I think about it. I guess she also mentioned her parents?"

Her parents? Why hadn't he thought to ask her about her family?

Before he could answer, Darcy plunged ahead. "In less than twenty-four hours, she lost everyone who mattered most in her world. How she made it through that without completely coming unglued still boggles my mind. And to think that she's turned it into a way to help others..." Darcy's words trailed off, and she looked up at him. "Uh, she did tell you all this, right?"

He shook his head slowly from side to side, his eyes filling with unexpected tears. He swallowed against the knot in his throat. "Her parents were killed on the same day?"

Darcy nodded slowly, her face pale. "Yeah. Holly called them after Bruce dumped her, completely broken-hearted. They packed up and headed to the city to be with Holly, but they were killed in a car accident on the way. That's why the holidays are always so hard for her."

The room seemed to spin out of control, and Ian found a post to lean against, his legs shaking uncontrollably. The sleigh ride. No wonder she'd gotten so curt with him about how she kept a positive spin in spite of her losses. And then she'd grown quiet when he mentioned that at least he and Ella had time to say their goodbyes to Amy. Holly hadn't had that luxury. "Why didn't she tell me?"

Darcy hurried to his side. "First off, please don't mention it to Holly that I told you all this. I'll find a way to tell her that I accidentally let it slip. She's used to that about me. Now to answer your question, she didn't tell you because that's not her style. She's always been one to suffer silently and somehow completely cover it up, so that no one around her, including me, knows exactly how much she's struggling. Surely you've figured at least that much out."

Ian nodded his head sadly. "Yeah, I always accuse her of not being real, of being a little too chipper. Now I know what's behind it." He brought both hands to his face, and released a heavy sigh.

Darcy grew uncustomarily quiet. When he looked over at her, her eyes were searching his face once again. "You really care about her, don't you?"

There was no use denying it. "Yes, I do." He lowered his head and blew air from puffed out cheeks. "We're all struggling with it. Ella. Me. But especially Holly."

"It's a mixture of her personality and life experiences that makes her that way, Ian, so be patient with her. She's gun-shy and running scared."

The perfect way to describe her. "You seem to have her pretty well pegged. Are you a psychologist too?"

Darcy laughed and returned to the rack of clothes, laughing out loud. "Me? Not a chance, though I do consider myself a student of human behavior. I'm a writer."

"Oh, really? What do you write?"

She raised her gaze to his, a devilish grin on her face. "Romance novels." She sent him a wink. "Thanks for all the fodder. Just what I needed to break my writer's block."

Ian felt his face pale, grateful that he was still leaning against the post.

Darcy called over to him. "You okay?"

He nodded.

"I'm going to go pay for this, then we can go find Holly and Ella."

As they exited the store a few minutes later, Ian found the courage to ask Darcy the question ricocheting in his brain. "As Holly's friend, how would you suggest that I handle things?" She stopped in her tracks, forcing his gaze to hers. "You've got to draw her out and make her talk, Ian. If not, she's gonna burrow down into herself so deep that you don't stand a chance. Whatever it takes, even if it means making her angry, you've got to get her to talk."

Ian looked up at the Christmas decorations hanging from the mall ceiling. How in the world was he ever going to accomplish such an impossible task?

Eleven

Later that day, Holly looked up as Darcy made her way down the stairs. "Did you get all settled in?"

Her friend smiled, dramatically rolling her eyes for effect. "Did I ever! This place is gorgeous. I could get so much writing done here."

Holly laughed and patted the couch. "Come sit down, and let's catch up. You know you're always welcome to stay as long as you'd like."

"Maybe on this end, but my boss would object big time. Some of us have to work in the real world, you know."

A frown creased Holly's forehead.

"I'm sorry, Holly. I didn't mean that the way it sounded. Blame it on jet lag. One of these days, I'll hopefully land a multi-book deal, and then I can leave the moonlighting life behind."

"There's not a doubt in my mind that it will happen, Darcy. You're an excellent writer."

"Yeah, me and every other person on the streets of New York City." She paused briefly. "Including their dogs."

Holly laughed. "I've met lots of nice dogs, but not one that even came close to writing as well as you."

Darcy skewed her lips to one side. "Hmm, maybe that's an angle I should try. Writing as a dog. Others have done it successfully."

They shared a laugh, then Holly could no longer hold back the question she'd been reining in since they arrived back in Evergreen. "So what do you think of Ella and Ian?"

Her friend looked her full in the face, her own face soft and smiling. "They're wonderful, Holly. They really are. I can see why you're smitten with both of them."

"I'm not smitten with Ian."

Darcy rolled her eyes. "Oh, puh-lease, girlfriend. This is me you're talking to, remember? You've got smitten written all over your face."

Holly froze in terror. "Really? I don't mean to."

"Oh, relax. I'd be smitten too, if I were in your shoes. You two are MFEO for sure."

"MFEO?"

Darcy gave her a "what-rock-have-you-been-hiding-under" look. "Really, Holly? *Sleepless in Seattle*? Meg Ryan and Tom Hanks?"

Holly shook her head, completely dumbfounded. "I'm clueless in Evergreen, as in I don't have a clue what you're talking about."

"You've never seen the movie *Sleepless in Seattle*?"

Holly shook her head. "Should I have?"

"It's only one of the best romance movies of all time. But that at least explains why you don't know what MFEO means."

"What does it mean?"

"Hello. Made for each other."

The frown returned, and Holly stared out the window. Made for each other? Was that God's plan, or was it just wishful thinking?"

"Ian cares about you, Holly."

"Maybe." But even as she spoke the word, she knew the truth of her friend's statement. And wasn't that exactly what she was trying to avoid?

"And as I already mentioned, you're smitten."

Yeah, definitely. She heaved a sigh. "Neither of which really matter under the circumstances. They're my clients."

Darcy returned to making her overly-dramatic faces and gestures. "As you've said ad nauseum on the phone ever since you got here. They might be your clients now, but they won't always be."

"Yes, but by then I'll be back at home in the city."

"But you don't have to be, Miss I-Can-Work-From-Anywhere." Her eyes narrowed. "Wanna know what I think?"

"Not particularly."

"Well, I'm gonna tell you anyway. I think you're just making excuses because you're scared."

The words hit Holly's brain like a hammer on a nail. That would be true. "Yes, I am." The words came out, but they were soft and subdued. "And I have good reason to be that way."

"Just another excuse."

Holly's mouth opened and her eyes widened as she glared at her friend. "You of all people should understand what I've been through. That's enough to make anyone cautious."

"Cautious? Is that what you call it? That's not caution. That's fear. On steroids!"

Holly leaned forward, elbows on knees, and planted her face in her palms. "Besides that, he doesn't believe in God." Even though she had hope that was changing.

"At least not at the moment." Darcy spoke the words, then scooted close and wrapped both arms around her, enveloping her in a sideways hug. "Oh, Holly. I don't mean to hurt you. I love you and want you to be happy."

Holly leaned back to look at her friend. "I'm a total mess, aren't I?"

"Yes, honey, you are." She gave Holly's cheek a playful pinch. "But you're a loveable mess."

"Ian's always telling me that I need to practice what I preach."

"I knew I liked that guy. He's got you pegged."

"Yeah, I know. Just one more thing that makes me even more smitten with him. How do I handle this, Darcy? I'm scared of getting too close and then things falling apart. Yes, it would hurt me, but it could destroy Ella, and I just can't let that happen."

Darcy laid a hand on her shoulder. "Can I give you some of your own advice?"

"Mmmm, I guess so."

"Get out of your head. It's not your job to figure it out. It's your job--" Her friend intentionally stopped so Holly would have to finish the comment.

"--to trust the Lord."

Darcy sent a proud smile. "Exactly."

Holly heaved a sigh. Now if she could only learn to follow her own advice.

The next morning, Darcy and Holly met Ian and Ella outside the doors of Evergreen Community Church. Ian had to force his jaw shut to keep it from coming unhinged. He'd never seen Holly look so dressed up and beautiful.

She smiled at him as she smoothed down an imaginary wrinkle in her clothing. "Sure hope I'm dressed okay."

"You look gorgeous, I mean, nice. You look really, really nice." His nerves and his pulse began an odd little dance.

About that time, Ella waved to a friend. "Dad, can I sit with Sarah during church?"

Unsure of what to do, Ian sent Holly a nonverbal plea for help.

She smiled at him and nodded.

"Sure, sweetheart. Just look for us afterwards." He turned to watch Ella do a half-skip, half-run across the parking lot.

Holly came and stood beside him, Darcy on the other side of her. "She's okay, Ian. This is some of that freedom that we talked about giving her."

"I know. It's just hard to let her go." He watched his daughter disappear through the front door of the church. "Well, I guess we'd better go on inside." Holly didn't budge, but neither did he. Was she as nervous about this as he was?

"Yeah, I guess so."

Darcy took off toward the building. "You two can stand there and be nervous Nellies if you want. I'm freezing to death."

Ian laughed. Leave it to Darcy to call it like she saw it, and ease everyone's tension in the process.

Once inside, Ian was surprised to find people milling around in a large open space, laughing and talking. Off to one side was a coffee bar, and beside that sat a round table loaded with food. Music played in the background. Everyone was friendly and smiling and seemed to truly enjoy being there. Much different than what he'd grown up with.

Holly's face lit up brighter than any Christmas tree he'd ever seen. "I like this place. This is exactly how I believe church should be."

Just as she finished speaking, a voice sounded from the nearby sanctuary. "Good morning, everyone! We're about to start our worship service, so please make your way to a seat. It's okay to bring in your drinks and food. We want you to feel like you belong here. Please make yourself at home."

People poured in through several opened doors that led into the small auditorium. A band began to play on stage as people quieted down and found a place to sit. Then, in another minute or so, a woman with a guitar in her hands moved to the microphone and started singing. The words she sang were projected onto a large screen. All around him, people joined in, including Holly.

The sound of her singing stirred a place deep within Ian's soul. But it was the light gleaming from her face that tipped him over the edge, and within a few more minutes, he found himself singing along. He spotted Ella a few rows ahead, standing next to Sarah and her parents. She was singing as well, her hands and face lifted toward the ceiling. Without warning, his eyes flooded with tears. What was happening to him?

The worship music ended all too soon for him, but he followed Holly's lead and took a seat.

A thin older man, dressed in blue jeans and a button-down shirt, moved to the center of the stage and began praying. "Lord Jesus, thank You for the opportunity to once more join together in lifting our praise to You. You alone are the true and living God, and You alone are worthy of all our praise, worship, adoration, devotion, majesty, splendor, glory, and so much more. Bless our time together in Your Word. Help us to quench our thirst for You this morning by allowing our spiritual roots to soak up Your presence and the message You have for us. As you have blessed us, help us to in turn bless others. In the strong name of Jesus, we pray. Amen."

He began reading from his Bible, the words also on the screen. "*How blessed*--in the original Hebrew that means happy and rejoicing--*how blessed is the man who does not walk in the counsel of the wicked*--that means he or she doesn't seek their counsel and advice--*Nor stand in the path of sinners*--which means they don't adopt the ways of the world--*Nor sit in the seat of scoffers*--joining those who are scornful of God."

He paused and looked up. "Did you notice the progression there? First this person is walking and seeking counsel from places that could get him in trouble. Then he stands in the path with them, adopting their ways. Then he sits, and joins them in scoffing at God. This shows us just how easy it is to get off track in our spiritual lives, doesn't it?"

Ian thought back on his own life. Hadn't his life followed this very pattern? Could it be that the Bible was true? That it really was a manual for living?

The pastor resumed his reading of the scripture. "*But his delight is in the law of the LORD, And in His law he meditates day and night.*" He looked up and smiled a smile that lit his face from within. "Folks, we need to delight ourselves in the Word of God." He held up his Bible. "It's a treasure trove of useful and blessed information. Even better, it teaches us about God and His Son Jesus. It's the most scrutinized book in the history of the world and has passed the test time and time again. Now back to the passage. *He will be like a tree firmly planted--*in other words, transplanted, *by streams of water, Which yields, or produces its fruit in its season And its leaf does not wither."* He looked up again. "I love that part. He's talking about a tree that is always flourishing. One that is evergreen because its leaves don't wither." He turned back to his Bible. *"And in whatever he does, he prospers."*

Ian stole a glance at Holly, and his pulse quickened. Never had he seen her more radiant and beautiful. Wasn't she just like the tree the pastor was describing? She seemed to have an endless supply of nourishment that sustained her. Maybe that's why she always seemed genuinely happy and upbeat and positive.

"Now we get to the comparison part, where the psalmist shows the difference of those without God. But before we go on with the passage, I think we need to remember that the only difference between the righteous and wicked mentioned in this passage is their relationship-- or the lack thereof--with God. Without Him, we're all in the same sad condition. Let's read again. *The ungodly are not so, But are like the chaff which the wind drives away. Therefore the wicked will not stand in the judgment, Nor sinners in the assembly of the righteous. For the LORD knows the way of the righteous, But the way of the wicked will perish."*

He faced the congregation once more. "Did you notice that the psalm started with 'blessed' and ended with 'perish?' Those two simple words sum up this entire passage, repeating a theme found throughout the Bible. Our time on earth offers two different paths--one with and one without God--with two very different outcomes. The path with God is one of blessing. The path without Him ends with perishing."

Ian licked his lips and swallowed around a huge knot of emotion that had stuck in his throat, his eyes trained on the man in front of him, his heart full of awe and wonder, but also doubts and fears.

"Think about chaff. It's just a dry husk, once close to the kernel. With that kernel, it's alive and flourishing like that tree we talked about. But without the kernel, it falls off and blows away to perish." He took a step closer to the front of the stage. "But this sermon isn't about the wicked or the chaff. I want our main focus to be on the blessing, because I've noticed an alarming trend among believers. One that must be addressed."

The room had grown so still and quiet that every little sound seemed magnified.

"We've entered the Christmas season, a joyous time to be sure. It's easy to get caught up in the holiday traditions. And there's nothing wrong with that as long as we don't let it become the main thing. Sometimes we humans have the tendency to receive a blessing--like the blessing of Jesus, God in the flesh, coming down to save us--and hoard it for ourselves."

He shook his head from side to side. "But the passage we just read shows us that we can't hoard it to ourselves. After all, the tree doesn't eat its own fruit, right?"

Murmurs sounded around the hushed and darkened room.

"No, we pass the fruit on to those who need a blessing." He stopped to allow his words to sink in. "We pass the fruit on to those in danger of becoming nothing more than bits of blowing chaff destined for the fire." His voice cracked with emotion and took on a pleading quality.

"You see, Jesus didn't come for Himself. He came for each of us." He stepped down from the stage to the same level as the congregation. "If you've received the blessing Jesus came to offer, your job is to be a channel of blessing by sharing Him with others. If you're here today and have not accepted that blessing for yourself, we'd love the opportunity to talk with you about doing just that. You can come during the invitation, or you can call the number on the screen at any time, day or night. Or maybe you know someone here that you feel more comfortable talking with. I know that they want to share the blessing of faith in Jesus with you."

The music once more resumed, and the congregation rose to their feet. For Ian, it was the oddest sort of sensation that he felt during that time. Like time stood still, but also like it rushed by in a torrent. But all he really knew was that he wanted Holly to be the one who answered his questions and shared the blessing.

Holly stood next to Ian and waved at Darcy one last time before she boarded the plane. For some indefinable reason, she almost wished that she were headed out as well. But why? She'd truly come to love Evergreen, and attending church yesterday had only cemented that feeling. And then there was her work in helping both Ian and Ella resolve their hurt.

"You ready to head on back to Evergreen?" Ian spoke the words from right behind her.

She turned to face him, trying her best to remain upbeat. "Sure."

A slight frown creased the area between his brows. "You okay?"

"Yeah." The look on his face showed that this was one of those times that he didn't believe her. "I'm just feeling a little sad to see Darcy go. I've spent the last couple of Christmases with her and her family, so--" She stopped abruptly, suddenly wishing she hadn't shared that information.

"So?"

"Never mind. Let's get back to Evergreen before you have to go to work."

"I'm off today, and Miranda is picking up Ella from school."

Holly's eyes widened. "Oh. Well, I guess we can use the time on the way back home to talk about a few more things."

"I'd like that. I, uh, have some questions."

She started walking down the hallway, occupying herself by searching for the signs that would lead them back out to Ian's car. "Okay. I have a few questions, too. Not just about Ella, but about when your parents will be arriving."

"Thanks for the reminder. Mom called last night and wanted me to ask you if they could come in later this week for some extended time with me and Ella."

Holly gulped down the wave of panic that hit immediately. "Um, sure."

Ian smiled knowingly. "Don't worry. I'm at your beck and call to do whatever needs doing to make that happen, including putting up the outdoor decorations."

A sigh of relief escaped Holly's lips. "Thank you. You must have heard the panic in my voice."

He winked. "Only slightly."

In a few minutes they pulled away from the airport and made their way back to Evergreen.

Holly looked over at him once the traffic thinned a bit. "Do you mind if I ask you a few more questions about Ella? I meant to ask them the other night, but I was in a bit of a funk."

"It's okay. I don't mind answering more questions."

"Thanks. I've been wondering about how well she's sleeping."

He sighed. "Not well. She doesn't seem to have trouble going to sleep, but she has trouble staying that way. I think she might be having trouble turning her brain off."

"Entirely likely." Hadn't she seen the same problem with other clients? "What about you? Do you sleep well?"

He seemed lost in figuring out the answer for a few minutes. Finally he spoke. "I hate to admit it, but I don't sleep well either. Sometimes I lay in bed awake for what seems like hours."

"I have a few tricks in my bag that might help both you and Ella, but you'll probably want to run some of them past your doctor first."

"At this point, I'm open to all suggestions."

"The first trick might sound counterintuitive, but it really does work. And I'm speaking from my own experience as well as hundreds of my clients."

He nodded.

"Don't lie in bed for over thirty minutes awake. Instead, get up and read in a quiet, dimly-lit place until you start feeling sleepy again."

"Why?"

"Because if you stay in bed wide awake, you start to associate your bed with wakefulness."

"Now that makes sense. Sometimes when I get ready for bed at night, I stare at my bed like it's the enemy."

Holly laughed. "Been there, done that. Had the bags under my eyes to prove it."

Ian's laughter joined hers. "But you're sleeping better?"

"I am. I'll be the first to admit that it's not always perfect, but I'm doing so much better."

"Good to know."

Holly chewed her bottom lip, sending up a quick prayer for help with bringing up this next tip. How would he react? "I've made myself a set of Bible verse cards that help me get my mind off of anxious thoughts. That's what I read when I can't sleep. It's been my experience that they help me more than any other strategy I use."

He pursed his lips, once more deep in thought. "Okay. Next tip?"

Well, that hadn't gotten her as far as she'd hoped. "Make sure to get plenty of sunshine, especially early in the day. That helps your body produce serotonin which is necessary for the production of melatonin to help you sleep at night."

"Last time I took Ella to the doctor, he suggested a medicine to help her focus and a different one to help her sleep. What are your thoughts?"

"I don't mean to go against your doctor. Some kids might truly need that approach."

He sent a sideways glance. "But?"

"But I think it makes more sense to try the natural approach first. Synthetic drugs aren't always the best option, and that's especially true for children since their brains are still developing."

He breathed out a sigh of relief. "That was exactly how I felt, so I'm glad your advice matches my initial instinct. Any other tips?"

"Tart cherry juice is sometimes helpful. Just a couple of ounces later in the day can help. Also try to have her eat her evening meal at least three hours before bedtime. Eating too close to bedtime can cause blood sugar spikes which can interrupt sleep. Make sure her room is as dark and cool as possible. I'd even take out electric devices, including alarm clocks."

"Really?"

"Our brains and bodies have an electrical component to them. Outer sources of electricity surround us all the time, and I personally believe they interfere."

A look of shock covered his features. "I never really thought about that, but it totally makes sense."

"There isn't a way to completely get away from electro-magnetic fields, but we can certainly minimize our exposure as much as possible."

For the next several minutes, Holly also coached him on optimal nutrition and stress management and their effect on sleep.

His eyes started to glaze over.

She chuckled. "I'm sorry. I know it's overwhelming. Don't let it stress you out though. Just make one small change at a time. I think you'll start noticing a difference in a fairly short amount of time."

"Can you give this to me in written form? I'm afraid of forgetting something."

"Absolutely."

The car grew quiet for several long minutes. Holly sneaked a sideways glance at Ian, who chewed the inside of his cheek. "Something bothering you?"

"Oh. Yeah, I mean, I, uh, wanted to ask you about something."

"Okay. Go ahead."

Ian looked more uncomfortable than she'd ever seen him before. "That's the problem. I'm not quite sure how to ask it."

"Just start talking your thoughts out loud. I promise to come to your rescue."

He smiled over at her, his eyes twinkling. "Thanks for taking it easy on me." He took a deep breath. "Yesterday at church, at the end of the service."

She inhaled, doing all she could to control her breathing. Was this the opportunity she'd been praying for? "When the pastor was talking about the blessing?"

"Yeah. Would you mind explaining it?"

Holly sent him a smile that seemed to put him at ease. "I'd be honored and delighted. First off, the blessing was Jesus coming to earth to save us from our sins. By doing so, He did something we could never do for ourselves."

"That's one thing that I've always kind of had trouble with. I mean, I'm not perfect, but I'm a pretty decent guy."

Holly laughed. "Well, except for trying to kill me."

He grimaced. "Oh yeah, well there is that."

"The truth is that God is perfect and holy. He cannot abide sin, and we can't stop ourselves from sinning. There are no levels of sin. One is just as bad as the other in God's eyes. So He became sin for us and took the punishment we deserved."

"Why would He do that?"

"Because He loves us and because He wanted to make a way for us to be in relationship with Him."

He grew pensive again. "It's the weirdest thing."

"What?"

"It all seems so simple and yet so mind-blowing, all at the same time. How do you know it's true?"

Gratitude filled Holly's heart. Had she not been through her own struggle with believing God after she lost her parents, she would never have been prepared to answer. "Lots of reasons. First off, I believe the Bible is God's Word and His way of revealing of Himself to man. It's historically accurate. There are archaeological evidences and scientific facts that back it up. And it was written over a span of 1500 years by over forty authors, all of which attest to the same truths."

A sense of awe descended on his heart. "Another mind-boggling statement."

Holly nodded. "In my own personal experience, He's as real--no, even more real--than all we see around us. I feel Him in my heart, and I sense His Presence with me. I know that might seem hard to believe, but it's true."

Ian looked over at her, sincerity resonating in his face. "In some ways it is hard to believe, but I also see how strong you are, like you're connected to some unseen energy source."

Her heart pounded at his words. *Father, thank You for Your living water within me that flows out of me and onto others. Help Ian to reach the place where he also receives the blessing of Jesus. Give me words that will lead him to You.*

He looked over at her. "Sorry if I embarrassed you."

"I'm not embarrassed. I'm grateful."

For a few minutes he was quiet, and Holly used the time to pray even more fervently.

At long last, Ian broke the silence. "So what do I need to do to get that blessing?"

"What do you normally do when someone offers you a gift?"

"I take it." Once more he descended into deep thought, but when he spoke again, it had nothing to do with receiving the gift--the blessing--Jesus offered.

At first, Holly felt overwhelming disappointment. But as she prayed through it, one thought brought consolation.

At least the seed had been planted.

Twelve

Holly couldn't help but smile as she made her way to the living room to where Ian's mom, Valerie, sat. The decorations looked even better than she'd hoped for, and her lengthy to-do list was now ta-done, thanks to Ian's tireless efforts. Then why was she still so melancholy? While it was great to be with Ella, Ian, and his family, she almost felt like a little girl with no money, standing outside the store and staring into the window at the one thing her life was missing. At the one thing she couldn't afford. Holly handed Valerie a cup of spiced tea and sat down next to her to help with wrapping gifts.

Valerie smiled over at her. "Thank you for opening your temporary home to us for the holidays." Her eyes scanned the beautiful cabin. "This place is stunning, and I love what you've done with the decorations."

"I went a bit overboard, but there's something about being in Evergreen that brings out the kid in me. Plus Ella was so excited to help, and I think I must have run Ian ragged with all that I asked him to do." She stopped short of saying that the holidays were something she'd dreaded because of her own losses. That was beside the point anyway. And so far, the Christmas season had been so much better than she'd expected. She sent yet another quick thank you spiraling to heaven's gates.

Ian's mom smiled, but turned her focus on the gift she was wrapping. "There is another thing I wanted to thank you for."

"What's that?"

"For bringing Christmas back into their lives. We've tried, but ever since Amy died, almost two years ago to the day, it's like Christmas became a reminder of her and their loss rather than Jesus."

Jesus? Were Ian's parents believers? "Forgive me for asking, but I'm guessing by your comment that you're a believer?"

"Absolutely, and so is Ian's dad."

Holly frowned. How could she ask the question that burned inside her without overstepping her bounds.

"You look as though you have a question."

"Yes, but I'm not quite sure how to ask. So please forgive me if I'm being too personal."

Valerie sent a reassuring smile. "It's okay. Go ahead and ask."

"It's just that Ian's not a believer--"

"--and you're wondering why?"

"Yes."

"I wish I knew that answer myself. He was raised in church, but never fully accepted what we believed and taught. Then when Amy died, it was like he completely turned his back on the idea of God."

Holly nodded. "He and I have talked about it, and that's exactly how he described it."

Valerie suddenly looked very sad, and tears welled in her eyes.

Holly's heart went out to her. She reached over and placed a hand on her arm. "But I truly believe he might be coming around."

The older woman smiled, hope now residing in place of the sorrow. "Really? What makes you think so?"

Holly recounted their conversation on the way back from dropping off Darcy at the airport. "Even though he didn't seem to make a decision one way or the other, I do think he's giving it lots of thought."

Valerie raised a grateful gaze to the ceiling, as though sending up thanksgiving. "Thank you for sharing that with me. We've been praying for it for years."

"And I've joined you in that prayer. Do you ever discuss it with him?"

The woman inhaled sharply. "Probably not as much as we should. But the last time we tried, he got very irate. At that point, we both questioned if it wasn't better just to try a different approach. He knows where we stand." Valerie finished taping up a gift and sat it to one side. "At least Ella believes. And she seems to be doing so much better than when we saw her over the summer."

Relief washed over Holly at her words. "I'm so glad to hear that. Based on how Ella responded to helping me decorate, I think it's been a healthy way to heal from that loss and remember happy times with her mom."

"I agree, but Ian...well, that's a different story."

Holly winced. In trying to help Ella had she deepened Ian's pain? Had he changed for the worse?

Valerie's words interrupted her thoughts and questions. "Christmas has always been an important part of our family celebrations. But ever since..." Her words dwindled away.

The pain etched on Valerie's face unleashed daggers on Holly's heart. She reached over and placed a hand on the woman's arm once more, drawing her gaze. "That must have been so hard."

"It was. Since then, Ian seems so lost. And protective of himself and Ella."

"I can certainly understand that." And hadn't she experienced it to a degree? Was it anything short of a miracle from the Lord that he'd ever agreed to let her help at all?

"Yes, but he can't stay in that place forever. He used to be such a free spirit, so full of joy. I wish with all my heart that he could get back to how he used to be. Oh, how I pray that he comes to know the Lord. I truly believe that would change things for him completely."

Holly nodded. "I totally agree. But I think it's important to also remember that the events in our lives--especially the tragedies and heartbreaks--sometimes change us so profoundly..." She lowered her gaze to hide her eyes, now brimming with tears.

Valerie laid a hand on her shoulder. "Spoken like someone who knows."

Holly's head raised sharply, and she locked eyes with Valerie.

The older woman smiled kindly. "If you ever need to talk about it, I'm a good listener."

Holly nodded, but once more lowered her gaze. Maybe some time, but not now. She couldn't allow herself that luxury with Ian, his dad, and Ella due back from the nighttime snowmobile ride at any time. That deep wound, unleashed by memories, always left her a soppy mess.

Later that evening, after Ella was in bed, Valerie came into the great room from the kitchen. "Ian, I need some things from the grocery store. Would you mind making a quick trip for me?"

Ian grinned at her, seeming very unlike the gruff Ian Holly had grown accustomed to. "Of course." He sent Holly a sideways look. "Want to make a grocery store run with me? You haven't been out of the house all day."

She nodded, taken aback. "Actually I would. The cabin fever is starting to set in."

Within a few minutes they pulled up outside the one and only grocery store in Evergreen. The lights were off, and there were no cars in the parking lot."

"Oh no. What are we going to do?" Holly looked over at Ian.

He pulled out his phone and started punching buttons. "No prob. I'll send Mom a text and we'll drive on down the road until we find an open store. That okay with you?"

"Sure. What's not to love about driving on a night like this one?" The bright-white full moon painted the snow a bluish silver, and the river running through town--along with the lake it spilled into--sparkled like diamonds.

Ian finished punching buttons and dropped his phone back in his pocket before putting his Subaru in reverse and exiting the parking lot. "That's why I've got to get you out on the snowmobiles on a night like this. You would love it."

"I'm sure I would."

"You could have come tonight."

"Yes, but I would have felt bad all night about leaving your mom alone at the house."

The conversation lagged for a second, but Ian looked over at her, his face and soft smile illuminated by the moonlit night. "That was very thoughtful of you. Thank you." He paused. "But I've noticed that you are pretty much always considerate and thoughtful when it comes to others."

"Thanks." She scrambled for a way to turn the conversation off herself to relieve her discomfort. "So have you always been a ski instructor?"

"Actually, no. Want to take a guess at my former career?"

She racked her brain, but came up empty-handed, mainly because there were so many things he would be good at. "I don't have a clue."

"I used to travel the country as an adventure guide and consultant."

"That sounds perfect for you."

"Yes, but not for my family."

A family man. Yet another reason to fall for him.

"When did you give it up?"

"After Amy died." His voice held pain. "She begged me for years to give it up so that we could all spend more time together. But I thought the money was too good to give up. Her death made me realize that there are so many more important things than money." He made a sharp turn to the left. "Ah, here we go. I knew we'd find an open store eventually."

As they did the necessary shopping, Holly didn't know whether to be relieved or sad that she hadn't had time to respond to his heartrending words. But things, including timing, didn't happen by chance, and she had to trust that God knew exactly what He was doing.

As they exited the store several minutes later, she decided to bring the topic back up once they were on the way home. But no sooner had they pulled out of the parking lot, Ian spoke first. "I've been meaning to ask how your business is going here in Evergreen."

"Oh, I forgot to tell you. I finally got internet service last week. It was tough doing it by phone or by driving to a place with free internet, but it worked."

"Glad to hear it."

Her thoughts took over. Should she be upfront with him about all she'd been thinking?

"You're sure being quiet. Something you need to talk about?"

She smiled over at him. "Very perceptive of you."

"That's usually your forte, not mine."

"True. Maybe I'm rubbing off on you."

He looked over at her, a soft glint in his eyes. "I can think of worse things that could happen."

Her breath caught in her throat. How she managed keep her expression calm and collected, she had no idea. The semi-darkness definitely helped. "Actually, once I got used to the shock of not having internet, I didn't miss some of my work as much as I expected. At least I still got to do the part I enjoy the most."

"Let me guess. Helping others?"

"Yeah, but I didn't miss the online promotion and blogging. Online entrepreneurial work is great, but you have to wear so many hats to pull it off."

"Hmm. Guess I'd never really thought that it was so involved. That explains why your lights are sometimes on until the wee hours of the morning."

Her eyebrows reached for her hairline. He'd been monitoring her awake hours? "If you were awake to see it, it means that you weren't sleeping either." She frowned.

"But I guess that's just one more example of how I encourage my clients to follow a lifestyle that I can't always keep."

"Don't be so hard on yourself. You're still giving good advice to folks. Just do the best you can." He paused, and turned his head toward her. "After all, you need to take care of your health and wellbeing too."

"I've actually been giving that a lot of thought."

"Oh?"

"Yeah. I've been thinking about opening a private practice somewhere and actually settling down. Traveling less. Staying put more." What was she saying? Would he interpret her words in the way she meant them?

He chuckled. "I've been thinking the opposite. Ella's to the age that she could learn so much by traveling more. But there is also her education to take into consideration. I don't know how I could tend to her schooling and go back to my former work."

Holly's spirits sank. So they weren't any closer to being on the same page. "She's definitely curious and adventurous."

He nodded. "Yeah. Much more than I realized, until...until you came."

She didn't respond verbally, but inside her spirits lifted. It helped to know she had made a difference. Had helped him see the possibilities. Even in small ways.

"One reason the nomadic lifestyle appeals to me is that I feel like somewhere along the way I lost the ability to see the world like a kid does. I miss that sense of wonder and adventure." He paused, then turned to face her, his light blue eyes illuminated by the moonlight. "But I think I'm learning that you don't have to go to new places to experience that wonder. It's a matter of choosing to see it."

She didn't respond, unsure of what to say.

"I guess what I'm trying to say is that I feel the wonder of Christmas this year. Something I haven't felt in a very long time."

Holly wanted to speak, but no words would come. Hadn't she felt the same way?

"And I think I have you to thank for it."

Her gaze locked with his, both excruciating and breath-stealing. Unable to hold his gaze, she turned to look out the window. "I'm glad to have helped."

That was it. Her lifeless words had completely stripped the magic from the moment. She searched for something to say, anything to break the now-deafening silence. "Speaking of wonder, I've been meaning to ask if you'd given any thought to our conversation on the way from the airport the other day. You know, about--"

"--I know what you're referring to, Holly. You don't have to spell it out." His voice held a frustrated edge that she hadn't heard from him in weeks.

Just a short while later, they pulled into the driveway, gathered their bags, and walked--without saying a word-- into the house.

Not long after they returned, Holly excused herself for the night and went upstairs.

Disappointed that his curt words had put a damper on the evening, Ian opted to spend some time reading instead. Just as he started to lower his weight to the couch his mom entered the great room. "Not so fast." He remained standing and looked her way. "Want to take a moonlight walk with your mother?" She paused and gave him the mother-evil-eye. "And if you know what's good for you, you'll say yes."

"Then yes it is. Let me get my coat."

A few minutes later they walked down the hiking trail behind Holly's cabin, the full moon on the snow giving them plenty of light to see by.

"Gosh, but it's beautiful here," said his mom. "I can't imagine a better place to spend Christmas."

"It is beautiful, isn't it? And it's almost like I'm seeing it with fresh eyes this year."

She sent a sideways glance. "Would that by any chance have anything to do with Holly?"

He nodded. "Yeah. In fact, it has everything to do with her. I never thought I'd feel this way again. It's exhilarating and scary at the same time."

"How is it scary?"

Ian released a heartfelt sigh. "She's a world traveler, and has built her business around taking it with her wherever she feels like heading next. I don't want us to ruin that for her."

"I don't think you would."

"What makes you say that?"

His mom was silent for a few moments. "We had a chance to talk a lot while you and Dad took Ella snowmobiling. She may not have told you about it. In fact, I'm betting that she hasn't. But I think she knows firsthand the kind of loss you and Ella have experienced."

A sudden rush of mixed emotions made his mouth go dry, and tightened his chest. Had she shared about her parents with his mom, but not him? Or maybe she'd just mentioned her former fiancé. "What did she tell you?"

"Not a lot verbally, but her face said plenty. It might be a good idea for you to try to find out what's going on. As much as she tries to help others heal, it appears she has quite a bit of healing to do herself."

"Yeah. We've talked about that before."

"About her needing to heal?"

"More like her needing to let others take care of her the way she takes care of them."

A soft smile played on his mother's lips. "It's good to see this side of you again, Ian. I want this kind of joy for you. Don't wait about finding out how she feels if you feel strongly about her. Never miss the opportunity to once more experience love." She reached through the semi-darkness and grabbed hold of his hand. "Overall, I'd say she's perfectly wonderful. A real keeper."

A real keeper. But what if she didn't want to be kept?

The next morning, Ian waited until Holly left the house to go on her morning exercise session, and then followed. It didn't take him long to catch up to her. "Mind if I join you?"

She didn't look all that excited about the idea, but she nodded anyway. "Sure."

"First I want to apologize for last night. I was a little short with you, and that was totally unnecessary."

"I shouldn't have interfered. So I'm sorry, too."

"I'm not ready to answer that particular question yet, Holly, but I do want you to know that I'm thinking through it and studying up on a few things. I'm actually surprised by how much I've forgotten since I was a kid." He looked over at her, but she continued to walk with her head down and her gaze averted. "I promise that I'll let you know when I'm ready."

She didn't respond other than to nod her head.

Now how could he turn the conversation to the matter his mother had mentioned? Maybe prayer would help. *Lord, Holly and I both have a lot to work through, and I could sure use Your help. Show me how to best approach this subject.* What was it Darcy had said? Something about getting her to talk before she burrowed down so deep inside herself that she wouldn't come back. He looked at her. Was it already too late?

At that moment they came to a clearing. Holly stepped off the path and moved to a large boulder. She dusted off the snow and sat down. "You go on ahead. I need some time alone to think through a few things."

Did he dare risk making her angry? After all, last night he'd basically told her to back off. Could he now turn around and not back off when she wanted him to? He released a heavy breath and moved to stand in front of her, looking her full in the face. "When someone you love dies, you feel like part of your own heart dies with them." Where had those words even come from?

Her eyes filled with unshed tears, but still she avoided his gaze. "I'm sorry you had to go through that."

Sudden understanding hit, corroborating the words of both his mother and Darcy. Holly knew not only the loss of love, but the loss and finality of death. Still suffered from its deep wound. The deep sorrow in her eyes proved the truth of his thoughts. He reached out and lifted her chin to meet his gaze. "Darcy told me about your parents."

She nodded. "She mentioned that she'd accidentally let a few things slip. I wondered if that's what she meant."

"I'm really sorry, Holly."

Holly pulled her head back and inhaled sharply, her eyes pooling with tears. "I really don't want to talk about it right now because I don't want to ruin the time with your family. Sometimes I get started crying, and I can't stop." She sat there a moment, head lowered and shoulders slumped, then once more raised her eyes to his. "It's enough to make you wonder if you can go on breathing. If your heart can ever beat again."

The forlorn look on her face ripped into his heart. Without even hesitating, his thoughts and prayers lifted toward God for His help. *Lord, help me get through to her before it's too late.*

Thirteen

That afternoon Ian stood at the kitchen window and watched Holly back out of the driveway on her way to some sort of musical rehearsal for the church's Christmas Eve service. As he pondered her earlier request not to talk about her loss, something inside of him broke open, unleashing a whirlwind of concern. Always focused on helping others, she'd stuffed her own heartbreak, packed it away in a tightly-sealed box, and stored it in the deep recesses of her heart. Instead of grieving as she needed to, she'd turned her pain into motivation to help others. A grand gesture to be sure, but at what cost to her?

He reached for his wallet, quickly retrieving the card he wanted. A few seconds later, he punched in the number from the card on his cell phone, then moved back to the couch while the phone rang.

"Hello?"

"Hi, Darcy. This is Ian. I need to ask you some questions. It's for Holly. I want to help her, but I need answers."

A heavy sigh sounded through the phone, followed by a lengthy silence.

He frowned. "Are you still there?"

"Yes. Look, I'll do my best to answer your questions, but this is thin ice we're both treading on. Holly is very sensitive about this kind of stuff, and it could backfire on both of us. But I love her dearly, and I want to help her too. What do you want to know?"

Almost an hour later, Ian ended the call and leaned his head back on the couch to stare at the darkened ceiling that flickered occasionally, reflecting the quickly dying fire. He pushed himself forward to stoke the fire, but only made it part way before the tears he'd been holding in during the phone conversation with Darcy unleashed in a torrent.

He wiped away tears, grateful that his parents had taken Ella to go sightseeing for the afternoon. It just wouldn't do for them to see him like this. Poor Holly. She'd experienced more suffering than most people even knew existed. Had been at the bottom of the heap. A pile of ashes kind of life. And somehow, in the midst of that kind of heartbreak, had overcome the odds and formed a massive business that helped no-telling how many people pick up their own pieces. Including him and Ella.

He thought back to the first day he'd met her and his stupid stunt on the ski slopes. In the next thought, all the times he'd ribbed her, or even been downright snarky about her Pollyanna personality. Had made her feel like a fake and a phony. Even wondered if she was one of many online leeches who preyed on helpless victims.

He'd been wrong on every single count. Why should she even give him the time of day after the way he'd treated her?

And yet, she'd shouldered it all and continued to do what she could to help him and Ella. And she'd succeeded.

Lord, I need Your help in returning the favor. Show me how to help her the way she helped us.

His eyes once more searched the flickering ceilings, waiting expectantly. Nothing came. He sat forward, head bowed, elbows on his knees. He'd just have to pray harder, because he somehow got the feeling that he didn't have much time left.

Three days before Christmas, the morning dawned bright and beautiful. Holly quickly donned her workout clothes and headed down the stairs, surprised to see Ian in front of the fireplace. She frowned and searched his face. It was lined with fatigue and his eyes bore tell-tale red rims. Not enough sleep, or something more?

A heavy sigh tumbled from her lips. Time was drawing short. She'd known it from the moment Ian's parents had arrived at the house. Her work here was nearly done, or at least as done as it was going to get. It had been a tough call to make, but there was no use in prolonging this agony for any of them.

Once Ian's parents left on the day after Christmas, she would also pack her things and leave. Already she'd made contact with Annie to let her know that she needed to find another house sitter.

But there was still one very important part of her work left undone. Like it or not, she had to talk to Ian about accepting the gift. She squared her shoulders and moved to the couch. "I'm about to head out for my walk. Want to join me?"

Total shock and surprise registered on his face. "Sure. Let me get my shoes on."

A few minutes later they were on the trail. Ian smiled at her as they walked beside the gurgling river. "Thanks for inviting me to walk with you."

"Honestly, I have an ulterior motive, but I don't think you're going to like it."

His lips clamped together, but he didn't respond immediately. "Okay. I'm guessing it's more questions about accepting the gift?"

"Yes."

He nodded. "Okay."

Holly's eyebrows shot up her forehead.

"But only if I can ask you some hard questions too."

She had no choice. "It's a deal. My turn first. What's keeping you from making the decision about Jesus?"

"First off, it's not something I want to rush in to. It's like the passage I was reading last night. I want to count the cost first."

Her jaw unhinged. "You've been reading the Bible?"

"Yes. I needed to know for myself if I thought it was true."

"So that's why you've been spending so much time with your nose in either a book or the computer."

"Yes."

Part of her felt guilty, but another part of her needed to push ahead, while it was still today. While she was still here. "I think that's very wise. Following Jesus is worth it, but it's also a sacrifice at times."

"How so?"

Okay, maybe she shouldn't have mentioned it. How could she answer his question without giving away the hurt in her own heart? "Sometimes following Him means saying 'no' to something else." She looked off toward the view of the valley and Evergreen stretching out in front of her. "Even something that you want very badly."

A dark frown descended on his face, but he didn't speak.

"Do you have any other questions or concerns about accepting Jesus as your Lord and Savior?"

"No." His direct gaze proved the honesty of his answer.

Well, so much for getting to the bottom of that issue. Could she leave not knowing the answer? The answer came immediately and in the form of yet another question. Did she have any choice? A non-answer was all the answer she needed. And sticking around was only going to make things more difficult for all of them.

"Okay, now it's my turn."

Holly breathed deep, doing her best to control her pounding pulse, but with no success. "Okay."

His eyes sent an apology that only served to increase her anxiety. "Forgive me for pushing, Holly, but this is one time when you need to let me help you."

Where was this going? And could she take it without falling apart, especially in her current emotional state? She somehow managed to keep a blank face, despite the fact that inwardly she'd already turned into a blob of Jello.

"What's your favorite Christmas memory of your mother?"

She flinched and her head quickly jerked his direction. "What kind of question is that?"

He shrugged. "An honest one." He held her gaze, refusing to back down. "I assume you have memories of your mother?"

"Of course." Even to her own ears, her tone was snappish.

They walked along in silence for a moment. Finally she released a heavy sigh. "Oh, all right. I don't necessarily want to go down this road, but if you insist."

"I do."

She fought against an instant wave of anger, fearful that steam and fire were about to shoot from her ears, eyes, and nostrils. But just as quickly, the anger subsided, replaced by tender memories of her mom. "Hmm, I haven't allowed myself to think about this in a very long time, but she always bought me a new ornament every Christmas, something to commemorate a special family memory that had taken place during that year."

"Do you still have the ornaments?"

She nodded, twisting her lips to one side to keep them from trembling. "I...uh...haven't taken them out of the closet since I put them there after the..." She clamped her lips together quickly, fighting back against a surge of tears that lay just below the surface.

"After the what?" His voice was soft, but firm. He wouldn't give up until he knew the answer. But if the floodgates burst inside her, was there any bringing it under control? "Why haven't you used them on your tree every Christmas?"

She tried to answer, but couldn't.

"Why, Holly?"

Exasperated, she turned on him, giving him the full vent of her fury. "Well, first off, you have to have a tree to do that."

He didn't respond, but he did keep his gaze on her, gently exploring and digging into her soul.

"Don't say it. I know. It's just another way that I'm a big fake and phony. I got you and Ella to start celebrating Christmas again, when I refused it for myself. It's just that..."

He stopped walking and faced her, placing both his hands on her shoulders. "I don't remember using the words 'big fake and phony' in my conversation with you today."

She pulled away and started walking again, and he fell into step beside here. "But I am a big fake and phony. I got you and Ella to start celebrating Christmas again. But in my case...well...it's just that..." She stopped, her gaze downward, and her face distorting with the distress she felt inside.

"It's just what?"

"Every one of those ornaments my mom gave me are like memories on branches." Her voice was choked and emotional.

"Yes, but part of healing from loss is allowing ourselves to remember the good instead of just rehearsing the bad." He paused. "Someone very wise once told me that."

Her face contorted, and he instinctively pulled her into a hug. "It's okay to let it out, Holly."

"I'm afraid to." She somehow choked out the words.

"I understand that fear. You know I do."

She could only nod, as there was absolutely no way she could speak without dissolving into tears.

"It's the fear that if you let go, you'll never find yourself again. But I'm here for you. You've helped me. Now let me help you."

That was all it took for giant sobs to explode from her in a heart-wrenching groan. But mixed with the grief from the loss of her parents was the knowledge that she was about to suffer yet another massive loss.

Ian eyed the clock on Christmas Eve. 6:00 p.m. The service was due to start at 6:30 p.m. His parents and Holly and Ella were already there, saving him a seat and expecting him to be there. He'd told them he was coming. Had met with the pastor earlier that morning without telling a soul. But now it felt like his legs were made of lead, like his whole body was refusing to cooperate. But why?

He raised his gaze to the ceiling, his heart crying out to God for help. In a matter of seconds, the weight lifted and the vise-like grip on his heart eased. "Thank You, Lord." Surely a spiritual battle for his soul had just taken place, and His Savior had emerged the Victor.

Now just one more thing to take care of before he left for the service.

First, he moved to the hall closet where Holly kept the Christmas wrapping paper. Then he moved back to the large box that had arrived at the post office earlier today. In a few minutes, he had the present wrapped, the bow on top, and the gift tag that said "To Holly, From Ian" peeking out from beneath the ribbon. Next he wrapped the smaller gift he and Ella had picked out together.

Now to get to the Christmas Eve service. A few minutes later, Ian pulled up outside the church and hurried inside, checking his watch as he half-walked, half-ran. He quickly scanned the congregation and saw three hands waving at him. He made his way through the crowded building and took a seat between his Dad and Ella. "Where's Holly?"

His mom smiled. "She's backstage, getting ready for her part in the program."

"Oh, yeah." How had he forgotten that she had a part in the music for tonight? And why had he forgotten to ask her about it? Yeah, he seriously needed to work on his communication skills, especially if his plan worked.

In a matter of minutes, the sanctuary lights dimmed, and the pastor stepped up to the microphone. "I'd like to welcome you all to our Christmas Eve service. I know we have guests, so let me tell you that we are so glad you are here. Let's begin with a word of prayer, and then we'll get started. Dear Father, thank You for loving us so much that you sent Your only Son to earth to be born as a baby, so that He could become the sacrifice for our sins." His voice broke, and it took him a moment to regain his composure. "Thank You for the special blessing--the special gift--of Your Son. It's that gift that we celebrate tonight, and it's in His name that we pray. Amen."

A huge spotlight shone on the center stage, where a man read from his Bible. Off to one side, a softer spotlight shone on a young couple dressed as Mary and Joseph, and cradling a baby. "...and she gave birth to her firstborn, a Son."

The woman playing the part of Mary, carried the baby as she stepped forward and music sounded from nearby speakers. When she looked up, Ian's heart landed in his throat. Holly! She began to sing. The song perfectly suited her voice, and her features were flooded with the wonder of

Christmas, that she could hold her newborn son who was also her Savior. "You're here. I'm holding you so near. You could have left us on our own, but You're here. Hallelujah, You're here."

Tears coursed, unchecked, down his cheeks. He swiped them away. What was happening to him? He'd cried more in the past two weeks than he had his entire life. As soon as the song ended, the pastor once more took the stage, Ian's cue to move to the baptistry.

On his way through the side door, he and Holly came face to face. He couldn't help engulfing her in a big hug. "Your song was beautiful." The words came out all hoarse, but he didn't care.

"What are you doing back here?" She pulled away and stared up at him.

"Um, well, it was supposed to be a surprise, but I'm being baptized. I accepted Christ as my Savior earlier today in the pastor's office."

Now it was her turn to hug him, her face more radiant than he'd ever seen it. "Oh, Ian, I'm so happy for you." Tears gushed from her eyes and down her radiant cheeks.

He raised a hand to brush them away. "I've got to go."

"I know. I'll see you afterward."

He moved past her, down the hall, and up the stairs to change clothes, the pastor's voice already sounding through the speakers. "It's easy to think of the baby in the manger and completely forget what He came for. He came for us because He loved us. He came to make a way for us to be in relationship to the Father. But that meant death and shedding of blood."

The heart-stirring words continued as Ian took his place at the top of the steps leading down into the water, his heart so full of true Christmas wonder that he could hardly breathe. Then, in just a few minutes' time, he went under the water to symbolize what Jesus had done and the new life within Him.

Holly woke up bright and early on Christmas morning, despite her poor night's sleep. She listened to see if she could hear anyone else stirring about, but the house was completely quiet. Good. Somehow she had to figure the mess of tangled emotions inside her, and the best way to do that was praying to the Lord in His Creation as she ran off some of the stress she felt inside.

After a quick peek out the window to see what the weather was doing, she opted for warmer than normal gear. She quickly changed and hurried downstairs and out the door, casting a quick glance at the living room to verify that her initial hunch was correct. The place was empty and quiet.

She hurried out the door. A fresh snow had fallen overnight, leaving the evergreens coated with a layer of white. How she hated to even ruin the smallest portion of this perfect snowfall with her footprints, but it was going to happen eventually. If not her, then another person would come along and leave their mark instead.

In less than a minute she was on the trail, enraptured by the stunning beauty around her.

Oh, Lord, how can I leave this behind?

As she jogged through the fresh snow, her mind immediately turned to Ian and Ella, especially the previous night, which in so many ways seemed like the culmination of her work. Ian had received Jesus. How the tears of joy had rolled down all their faces. Ella had seemed to transform from her sometimes moody self to the girl Ian had described before she lost her mother to cancer.

Her heart lurched in her chest, leaving a white-hot searing pain burning in her chest. *Lord, How can I leave Ian and Ella?* The same question that had kept her awake most of the night.

She released a puff of frosty white air, her shoulders sagging. "Not my will, Father, but yours. Show me what You want me to do." Out of nowhere, the verses she'd carried in her heart since right before coming to Evergreen, once more tugged at her memory and rolled off her lips. "*But blessed is the man who trusts in the LORD, whose confidence is in Him. He is like a tree planted by water, that sends out its roots by the stream, and does not fear when heat comes, for its leaves remain green, and is not anxious in the year of drought, for it does not cease to bear fruit.*"

The words seemed to have taken on new meaning in light of all that had happened. She'd trusted Him, even when she didn't understand, had jumped at the chance to be of possible help to Ella and Ian despite the possibility of a broken heart at the end of all this. But now, now she was facing a drought of heart that shook her to the core.

She slowed to a walk, breathing deep to catch her breath. Lifting hands and eyes to the gray skies and falling snow, she prayed out loud. "Father, forgive me. I belong to You, and You are always with me. I have no reason to fear. You love me. You have my best interest at heart, along with Your perfect plan and purposes. My life is Yours, not my own." A heavy weight lifted from her chest. "Help me to keep my eyes on You and not on what the future might hold for me." But even in saying the words, the potential for a lonely life stretched out before her life a dry, thirsty desert. "Even if it means a desert wilderness, Lord, I know You will walk that path with me."

The snow crunched behind her and she whirled about.

Ian stood in front of her. "Sorry. Didn't mean to startle you or interrupt your prayer." His face held a sad expression, or was it something else? How much had he heard?

As though reading her mind, his eyes grew apologetic. Ian lowered his head briefly. "I couldn't help but overhear you." A deep frown crinkled his eyebrows. "Are you leaving us?"

Her breath caught in her throat, razor-sharp. She swallowed against the pain. "That's what I'm trying to figure out." The words came out as an anguished whisper.

"If I stay, it's only going to get harder for all of us when I have to leave. I can't do that to Ella."

"But why do you have to leave at all?"

Was there a reason to stay? Ella and Ian needed time to find their relationship again, and her leaving would mean that could happen without any interference from her.

"What about Annie and John?"

She averted her gaze and released a breath from puffed-out cheeks. How could she tell him this? Would he understand? "I contacted them last week and asked them to find another house-sitter." She raised her gaze to his, fearful of what she'd see there.

His eyes and every pore of his face held profound hurt.

"I'm sorry, Ian, but I thought it was best."

He frowned and clamped his lips together for a long minute before making eye contact again. "Can't we talk about this together? Can't I have a say? And Ella?"

She shook her head sadly. "I'm just trying to do what I think is best for all of us. Surely you know that about me by now."

His whole expression softened. "Yes, but there's so much more to you that I know. I know you like exactly five marshmallows in your half-cup of hot chocolate, and that you only drink a half cup because you're trying to exercise self-control. I know you twist your hair with your right index finger when you're thinking hard about something. That you chew your bottom lip when you're upset, just like you're doing right now."

Her heart pounded in her chest and head, pulsing out a beat so loud she could barely think straight. What was he saying? And what did it mean?

A tender smile curved his lips ever so slightly. "What I'm trying to say, Holly, is that I've fallen in love with you."

An anguished sob shrieked from her lips. "That's exactly what I tried to keep from happening." She raised both mittens to her face to hide the deluge of tears.

But before she knew it, he was at her side, engulfing her in a bear hug that left her even more confused. On one hand, it offered comfort and the promise of something more, but on the other hand, it also held the potential for more heartbreak. A heartbreak that would surely be her demise.

Not everything that looks like a drought to you is actually a drought. Her sobs subsided. Where did that thought come from? Then she was aware of Ian talking to her gently. Had he spoken the words? And if so, how did he know about the verse God had etched on her heart and mind?

"I know it's scary, Holly. It's scary for me, too." He pulled away and looked into her eyes. "Remember when we talked about how you can't always plan for things like this, and that planning can rob everything of its beauty. You have to just accept it, the good, the bad, the possibilities either way, and you hang on for the ride. It can be exhilarating. And life-changing."

Yes. Already she felt the exhilaration, as though on a roller coaster headed for the steepest drop-off. She shivered, partly from excitement, but mostly from the cold. And the fear.

"Come on, let's get you inside by the fire. We can talk about this some more later."

She nodded, relieved that for now, they had postponed the matter. But as they made their way back inside, all her emotions once more hit critical mass, and she struggled to keep her focus on the Lord. That was the only way she'd be able to survive the drop-off ahead, no matter the final ending.

Fourteen

I an inhaled deeply as he passed out all the presents except the two he had tucked away behind the tree. Why was he suddenly a bundle of nerves? Was Holly's fear rubbing off on him? Or was his entire plan a huge mistake?

Ella came up beside him, the smile on her face bright and cheery enough to bring him encouragement. "We're not giving Holly the two behind the tree right now, are we?" She whispered the words softly so no one else could hear.

He gave his head a shake and sent her a wink. At least he and Ella were on the same page, but what about Holly? Could he and Ella survive it if she decided to return to New York? He breathed out a silent prayer for God's help as he and Ella handed out the last few presents. Then he moved over to his spot between Holly and Ella.

"We have a family custom of opening our gifts one at a time," he explained to Holly.

"Starting with the youngest!" Ella chimed in, her face full of excitement.

Holly's smile looked forced, and dark circles lay beneath her sad eyes. "I like this tradition. That means that you're up first, munchkin."

Ian interrupted. "But we're also starting a new tradition, beginning today."

Ella feigned a pout, then broke into a giggle.

Ian's heart skipped a beat as he smiled at her. The change in her was astounding. It was as though she'd turned a corner, once more back to her happy-go-lucky self. And he had Holly to thank for it. He met Holly's gaze, praying she could see the gratitude in his eyes.

She raised one eyebrow. "Um, the new tradition?"

"Oh, yeah. We're going to read the Christmas story in Luke 2." He turned to Ella. "Also something that the youngest gets to do. That is, if she can read."

His daughter made a face and then smiled. "I'd love to read it, but only if you promise to help me with some of those names."

Everyone laughed, and Ian's dad handed the Bible to his grand-daughter.

She rose and began reading. Instinctively, Ian stretched his hand over and place it on top of Holly's. He could feel her eyes on him, but he kept his gaze on Ella as she read. When she finished the passage, she turned to her grandfather. "Here you go, Poppy."

The older man's eyes were moist with tears. "Beautiful job, sweetheart."

Ella hugged both her grandparents and then returned to her seat.

Opening gifts took almost an hour as each person opened one gift and held it up for the others to see. When they were finished, Holly was the first to speak. "I really like that idea of going one at a time. It's really special."

Only Ian heard, because the other three had immediately left the room.

Holly watched their retreating backs, a frown darkening her face. "What's going on?"

Ian turned to face her and placed one arm on the back of the couch behind her. "I asked them to give me some time alone with you so we could talk."

A mixture of emotions crossed her face, but she didn't speak.

He looked at her directly. "Help me out here, Holly. I'm suddenly feeling like I'm on a raft in the middle of the ocean. In a storm. Without any oars."

Holly's face broke into a smile, and she even managed a soft giggle, lightening his heart. "Don't worry about it. It's just that thrill ride you're looking for."

Now it was his turn to laugh. "Guess I had that coming."

The tension between them had now dissipated. It was now or never. Ian took her hand in his own, and looked into her eyes. "I don't want you to leave. Neither does Ella."

"You talked to her about it?"

He nodded. "Of course."

She smiled her approval. "That was a very good thing to do."

"She actually helped me see some things that I hadn't considered." He paused and gave a slow wink. "Maybe you should try seeing some things you haven't considered."

She backhanded his arm.

"Ow!"

"Sorry. Just couldn't help myself."

He couldn't keep his eyes off her. Sheer delight seared through him, especially since she was maintaining eye contact. Surely that was a good sign. Ian reached up the hand that rested on the back of the couch, and brushed some stray strands of Holly's hair back into place. "Holly, I so look forward to getting to know you better. Please give us that chance."

Now her eyes took on sorrow. "I don't know, Ian. I'm just not sure it's wise at this point. What if we agreed to go our separate ways for a few months, to give you and Ella time to reconnect and..."

"There you go again. Trying to plan everything out."

She clamped her lips together, and her eyes held an apology.

Ian rose to his feet. "Sit here. I have a couple of things to get right quick." He moved behind the Christmas tree and retrieved both the small and the large packages.

As soon as she saw them, she protested. "Ian, you already gave me a gift. I didn't get you anything else besides the ornament I already gave you."

"It's okay. This is just something extra." He cocked his head to one side to look at her sideways. "My way of trying to convince you to stay."

She shook her head from side to side, as though exasperated. "You are devious, did you know that?"

"You should have figured that out the first day you met me."

"Now who's trying to control things?"

"My turn."

Her immediate laughter was contagious, and he couldn't help but join in. The laughter ended with them both sharing a glance that made Ian's heart sing. How was it that she could read his thoughts and share her own without saying a word? He handed her the smallest gift first. "This is something Ella and I had made for you. It comes with no strings attached. It's yours to remember us by, no matter what you decide."

"Thank you." She took the gift he offered and gently started unwrapping it without tearing the paper.

He couldn't help but chuckle.

She looked up, her eyes wide. "What?"

"Nothing. It's just that you even plan out how to unwrap your presents."

Holly sent a pretend evil eye and then unexpectedly ripped into the paper to get to the cardboard box."

"There you go. Live it up a little."

She laughed. "I have to admit it. That felt really good." She tore open the box and lifted her gift out of the box. "A snow globe. Oh, Ian..." Her eyes filled with tears, and he could tell she was having trouble speaking.

"I remembered what you said the night of the Christmas tree lighting ceremony, you know, about Evergreen reminding you of living in a snow globe. That's why we had the globe made by a friend of ours. There's our little cabin, and that's me and Ella standing outside. And behind us is the river with an evergreen tree standing right by the water." He looked over at Holly.

Her tears had subsided, replaced with a look of awe and wonder, and her eyes were fixed on the inscription at the bottom.

"Oh, I didn't ask him to put that on there, and I really don't know why he did, but I'm glad. It fits perfectly." He paused, then read the inscription out loud. "When the roots run deep, there is nothing to fear."

"It's beautiful. Thank you." Her tone was deep and throaty, and she seemed somewhat shaken and overcome with emotion.

Should he wait before giving her the next gift? If that one had touched her so much, what would the next one do? "Uh, want to wait on the next one?"

Holly swiped the tears from her cheeks with both palms and shook her head from side to side.

He handed her the larger gift next. "This one isn't from me, but it is to you. It's something that's been yours all along, but you've kind of kept it in the background of your life, afraid that it would hurt too much."

She frowned, but took the gift he offered. This time she didn't even bother trying to keep the paper intact, but ripped it off in a hurry, coming to a halt as she saw the box.

Her eyes widened, and she looked up at Ian. "Where did you get this?" Her voice held the same husky whisper.

"Darcy sent it to me at my request. We both think it's time." He pointed to the Christmas tree they had cut together on their outing with Ella. "I even cleared a place on the tree among all our ornaments."

Holly moved her gaze to the fire and raised her right index finger to her hair, twirling the strand around her finger over and over, totally lost in thought.

Ian's heart sank. So his plan had failed. Had his last gift backfired the way Darcy had said? He tried to breathe through the heavy ache in his chest, but it was so much harder than expected. "It's okay, Holly. I understand."

She stared at him, her gaze intently studying his face. "Do you really?" Her tone held an indefinable edge. Now she stood. "You stay here. I'll be back in a minute."

The sound of her boots against the hardwood floors grew softer as she left the room, and Ian allowed his shoulders to sag forward and his elbows to rest on his knees. It was a chance he had to take. Now he'd just have to pick up the pieces and move forward the best he could. *Lord, help me.*

Suddenly, he was aware of several pairs of footsteps behind him, and he turned to see Holly, Ella, and his mom and dad enter the room. He slowly rose to his feet, unsure of what to say or do.

Holly moved closer and picked up the box, facing all of them. "This box contains bits and pieces of my life. Bits and pieces that I hid away for way too long. But a friend of mine helped me see that I needed to face my fears so I could move ahead with my life." She allowed her gaze to meet Ian's and left it there for a long breath-stealing moment before turning back to the others. "But knowing that by opening it here that I am also making a scary but important decision, I'd like you all to help me please."

Ian's pulse quickened. But what exactly did that mean?

Holly inhaled deeply and released a shaky breath before setting the box down in front of the tree and kneeling down to open the box. Next, she smiled softly and reached inside, retrieving a golden ornament and hanging it on the tree. "This was the first ornament my parents bought together after they were married. To me it symbolizes steadfast love." She looked at Ian, her eyes aglow.

Unable to break his eyes away, he smiled at her, then rose to his feet and joined her at the tree. Within a few seconds' time, Ella joined them, followed by Ian's parents. They all talked and reminisced over each ornament, and then stood back, admiring the tree.

It was his mom who spoke first. "Ella, I could use the help of both you and your Poppy in the kitchen to help get ready for lunch."

Ella sent Holly and Ian a mischievous smile as she reached into her pocket. "Okay, but I want to leave this little present just in case you two need it." She laid something wrapped in tissue on the table and then followed her grandparents from the room.

Ian turned to Holly and held both her hands. "Don't leave us, Holly. We all want you here. Not for just one roller coaster ride, but for a lifetime of them."

"That's what I want too, Ian. And even more, I think it's what God wants for me." She looked over at the snow globe. "As soon as I saw the evergreen tree standing next to the river behind your cabin where you and Ella stood, and especially the inscription on the bottom, it was as though a verse God laid on my heart a few months ago came to life in a way I never expected." She lowered her gaze to their locked hands, and then a minute later, raised it back to his. "I don't know where all this will lead, but I'm willing to trust the Lord enough to see." Then she released his hand and pulled away, headed to the table. "But the suspense is killing me on what Ella wrapped in this tissue paper." She picked it up and quickly pulled the tissue off to reveal a sprig of mistletoe.

They both laughed, but then Ian moved to her side, took the mistletoe from her hand, and held it over her head. "I love you, Holly."

"And I love you."

The kiss lasted only a few seconds before Ian heard someone clearing their throat. Disgruntled, he pulled away to see Ella standing there.

His daughter stood with one hand on her hip and a questioning look resonating from her face. "Does this mean Holly's staying?"

"Yes." He couldn't help his grumpy tone, but he did manage a smile before he threw the mistletoe at his daughter and turned back to Holly for another kiss.

THE END

* * *

Thanks for taking the time to read *Evergreen*. I hope you enjoyed the story as much as I enjoyed writing it. If you enjoyed the book, please consider the following:

1. Join me in praying that all the books reach those who may need them for whatever reason.

2. Leave your honest review wherever you downloaded the eBook. This is a big help to other readers.

3. Share this eBook with those you think might enjoy it via your church or public library, as well as word of mouth, email, and social media channels.

* * *

Enjoy this sneak peek at the first book in the Miller's Creek series!

TEXAS ROADS
Chapter One

Dani's blue Honda Civic lurched and sputtered, drawing her attention to the neon-orange needle on the gas gauge. Empty. A frustrated growl rushed from her throat as she maneuvered onto the tufts of new spring grass at the side of the country road, turned off the ignition, and leaned her head back against the seat, berating herself for her forgetfulness. She'd love to blame this on the fight with her mother, but it wouldn't explain the hundreds of times she'd made similar mistakes—just one more to add to her collection.

She rubbed the dull ache building between her eyes and stared at her surroundings on this Texas back road. Why did she choose today, of all days, to visit her aunt, a woman she knew only from chatty letters and a brief phone call?

Escape.

She longed to escape. To disappear, to travel so far away that painful memories became yesterday's ashes.

A stray tear wandered down her cheek and she banished it with a swipe. Today marked the one-year anniversary of Richard's death. Death had robbed her—not only of her husband, but her dream—and stamped her heart's one desire with angry red letters: REQUEST DENIED. Thanks to the life insurance and inheritance of her father's company, a ridiculous sum of money now graced her bank account, but not enough to buy what couldn't be purchased. A house, yes, but not a home.

Stop wallowing, Dani. She grabbed her cell phone and flipped it open. No signal. Of course. She climbed from the car to scan the horizon. Nothing but tree-dotted pastures and a few cows. Breathing deep to quell the rush of panic, she closed her eyes and envisioned a sweet grandmother-type driving up to offer a ride. Her eyes fluttered open. Yeah, right. She wasn't Cinderella. Godmothers didn't exist. And Prince Charming? The biggest fairy tale of all.

Her marriage was proof.

Waiting to be rescued just squandered precious hours of daylight. She snatched her purse from the passenger seat, slammed the car door, and stamped toward Miller's Creek. Like a scratched CD, Mother's hurtful words from the earlier phone conversation replayed in her mind, and none of it made sense. Why did her mother oppose this visit to see Aunt Beth? And what had caused a rift the size of Texas between the two sisters?

A cramp commenced in her toes and inched into her feet. With a frown, she eyed her shoes. Heels weren't exactly the footwear of choice for hiking country roads. Balancing her discount-store purse in the crook of her arm, she rifled through its contents, searching for the keys as she marched back to the car. A sudden realization forced her into a stilted run, and a strangled sound ripped from her throat. "Please, no!"

The keys dangled from the ignition, teasing her like chocolate candy behind a counter of glass. With a guttural groan, Dani tilted her face toward the cloud-darkened sky. "What do You have against me?"

The isolated countryside responded with silence.

On the continued trek toward Miller's Creek, the hush enveloped her, the only sound an occasional bird's song and the rhythmic thud of her heels against the pavement. So peaceful, and so unlike the city's unending drone. The bluebonnets and Indian Blankets of early spring painted the countryside, stretching beyond the barbed-wire fence into open fields, and the breeze tangled her hair. As she breathed in the fresh air, her shoulder muscles unknotted. Then a low rumble pulled her gaze to the clouded sky.

Heavy raindrops pelted Dani's face and dotted her consignment shop designer jacket. Within minutes she was drenched, the metallic taste of make-up dribbling into her mouth. She kicked at a rock, self-pity seeping through her like the rain through her dry-clean-only suit.

With a shiver, she hunched over and pulled the soggy jacket closer in an effort to get warm. Burning pain in her left little toe hinted at the formation of a blister, but she hobbled on, her thoughts on her aunt. Could the woman provide the sense of family she so desperately needed? She attempted to toss the question from her mind. One thing was for certain. Her drowned-rat-appearance would make a memorable first impression. Just not in a good way.

The faint roar of an engine sounded behind her and intensified. Finally. She turned to see an older model pickup top the hill, and waved her arms in an effort to make herself seen in the rain and approaching nightfall. The beat-up truck slowed to a stop and the window lowered.

She tried to swallow, but her throat clamped shut. This was no grandmother. With one finger, a dusty cowboy pushed up his sweat-stained hat, his other arm draped over the steering wheel. "Can I give you a ride, ma'am?"

Dani brushed the drippy hair from her eyes, resisting the urge to correct his grammar. "I, uh . . . r-ran out of gas."

The cowboy smiled, his teeth white against his dirt-smudged face. "That's not what I asked."

With a glance in the direction of her car, her brain accelerated into high gear. "Actually, if you'd be so kind as to get me some gas—"

A soft chuckle resonated from him, and his eyes twinkled.

She hoisted her chin. How dare he laugh at her.

"Look, ma'am." His picture-perfect smile disappeared behind the long line of his lips, his voice laced with impatience. "I know you're concerned about accepting a ride with someone you don't know. Can't say I blame you. But by the time I get to town, get gas, and get back out here, it's going to be dark. Then you'll have plenty of reason to be afraid."

She raised a hand to her lips. What he said made sense, but could she trust him?

His mouth curled at the corners. "Coyotes are pretty bad in these parts. Sure wouldn't want to be out here after dark. Especially alone."

Coyotes? Dani yanked on the door handle and hoisted herself onto the grimy seat. After one breath in, she wrinkled her nose and sniffed. What was that smell? Eau de Sweat? She swiveled her head toward him and found his gaze trained on her, his face lined with suppressed laughter.

He needn't be so amused. She fidgeted with the seat belt and held it with one hand to keep it from riding across her nose. "I think someone up there must not like me."

"What makes you say that?" He stared at her like she was mentally unbalanced and put the truck in gear.

"It's just been a rough day. Like God has it in for me or something."

He raised one brow. "I think God must love you a lot, or I wouldn't have come home this way. Not many people use this road anymore."

Dani drew in a sharp breath. Did God love her? She gave her wet head a shake, sending droplets of water to the worn seat. No one could love her. Not even God.

Conversation lapsed as the rain continued its steady stream, thundering against the roof, yet unable to drown out the hum of the truck's engine. What would've happened to her if he hadn't driven by? The only coyotes she'd seen were in science videos at school. A surprising shudder scuttled down her spine, followed by a shiver that rattled her teeth.

The cowboy shifted her direction, his dark eyes focused on her ruined jacket. "You must be cold."

Brilliant deduction, Sherlock. Were all small-town people as intelligent as him? "What clued you in? My dripping clothes or blue lips?"

He laughed out loud, a hearty sound that made her somehow feel better. "Feeling a little testy, huh?" His eyes sparkled with amusement.

She hung her head, half in shame and partly to conceal the smile that crept onto her face without permission. "Sorry."

Dani started as he reached toward her, but relaxed when he pulled a brown suede leather jacket from behind the seat. "Here. This ought to warm you up."

"Thanks." She gripped the stained coat with two fingers, and examined it for signs of vermin. None that she could see. "Looks, uh...nice and cozy." She snuggled into its warmth and breathed in the light scent of men's cologne.

Richard.

She closed her eyes, the unwelcome memories and emotions clawing their way through her insides. The feelings still took her by surprise, crawling into her consciousness at unexpected times. Had she not been a good enough wife? Is that why he'd betrayed her, not just once, but several times? Her mind revisited their last fight. Richard had been more than happy to point out how many girlfriends he'd had during their ten-year marriage.

"By the way, I'm Steve Miller." The stranger's silky baritone interrupted her thoughts.

She opened her eyes to find his hand extended toward her. "Dani." She clasped his hand. Not as rough as she expected for a cowboy.

"You really shouldn't be on the back roads without enough fuel, you know." The look he gave her was stern, but kind.

Dani swallowed the sarcastic reply that popped into her head, and instead sent him a pasted-on smile.

His gaze rested on her wedding band. "Your husband not able to come along?"

The irony of his question made her grimace. At least the ring had served its purpose. She shook her head and focused on the passing terrain, some fields completely covered in wildflowers. How many more miles?

He leaned forward and made eye contact. "Been to Miller's Creek before?"

"Once when I was little, but I don't remember much about it."

"It's a nice place." His voice held a hint of pride. "Any family there?"

She slid a hand over her wet hair and cleared her throat. Time to change the subject and let him enjoy the hot seat for a while. "An aunt. What about you? Have you lived in Miller's Creek long?"

His eyebrow cocked into a furry question mark. "All my life."

"No surprise there," she muttered to herself. She glanced at his filthy blue jeans and tattered shirt. It had probably been that long since he'd taken a bath. Immediate guilt rained over her. *Ease up, Dani. At least he offered you a ride.*

"Excuse the way I look. We had a fence to mend today at the ranch."

Heat built up steam under her cheeks, and she averted her eyes. Okay, he wasn't supposed to hear that last comment.

His expression held nothing but friendliness. "I might know your aunt. What's her name?"

She rubbed fingers against her damp pants. Was it wise to divulge that information?

"Never mind." Steve held up a hand, a thin layer of black showing beneath his nails. "I know you city folks have to be careful about stuff like that."

What was it with his ability to read her mind? "City folks? You make it sound like a disease or something." She hugged her arms to her chest. "Besides, how do you know I'm from the city?"

"'Cause people from around here don't dress up in such fancy duds." His dark eyes glinted and her nerves unraveled more.

"True. They wear cowboy hats and drive beat-up trucks."

His throaty laughter reverberated in the cab. "Guess I had that coming."

Resting her elbow on the door, Dani leaned her hot face against her fist and wished for a punching bag.

"Which city?"

She stared at the tattered pickup cab ceiling and drew in a breath. "Dallas." If they didn't get to Miller's Creek soon she was going to blow.

"Should-a guessed that." Steve's face scrunched up.

"How can you stand living in the city with all that noise and traffic?"

"I suppose the same way you live with stinky old cows and a lack of civilization." Her voice rose in frustration. Dani immediately wished the blurted-out words back in her mouth.

She started to apologize, but Steve spoke before she could get a word out. "You in business for yourself, or you work for a corporation?"

Where'd he get that idea? "I'm an elementary school teacher."

"Really?" His brows notched up and he snickered.

Irritation seeped through the cracks of her frazzled nerves like floodwater penetrating a leaky dam. She twisted her head to glare at him. "Is that so difficult to believe?"

A smirk of a smile snaked across the cowboy's face. "Guess not. It's just that Miller's Creek teachers don't dress up like you. They get down on the floor with their kids."

The dam burst wide open. "Well now it's my turn to be amazed. I didn't know small towns like Miller's Creek had schools." She huffed out the words then yanked her head around to clamp a hand over her mouth. What was wrong with her today?

Broken only by the swish of the windshield wipers and the pit-pat of rain drops, the silence hung between them, thick and sultry. Suffocating. She let out a slow breath and ducked her head to study him from beneath her lashes. Steve faced forward, the dark hair at the nape of his neck curling upward, his stubbly jaw locked. Most of her friends would classify him as handsome, but she wasn't looking for a man. Not ever again.

He began to whistle, a shrill sound that chafed against her raw nerve endings. She pressed a hand to her temple. How much farther could it be? "Is there a convenience store in Miller's Creek by any chance?" She tried to infuse her tone with kindness.

His cinnamon eyes turned on her, dry hot winds that withered everything in their path. "Of course. Right next to the community outhouse."

A nervous giggle escaped before she could stifle it, but Steve's daggered glare brought it to a quick halt. After a few minutes she peeked at his face, now chiseled from granite. *Way to go, Dani.* She'd already offended one member of Miller's Creek and hadn't even made it to the city limits.

The rain ceased as they pulled into town, and she sat up straighter at the sight of country cottages lining the street. Homey. A little tired-looking, but nothing a fresh coat of paint couldn't fix. Tree branches arched across the road to create a living canopy. The sun, sandwiched between cloud and earth, changed the leaf-clinging raindrops to diamonds.

And children everywhere she looked. They splashed in puddles and chased each other across spring green lawns, their shouts and laughter a symphony of careless joy. So *Mayberry RFD.*

The hunger for home haunted her, and a familiar ache settled over her heart like ancient dust. "Unbelievable." Dani whispered the word and relaxed into the seat. The fear of never finding a home clung to her with razor-sharp talons, but she pushed it aside and glanced at Steve, his face impassive.

In one deft movement, he jerked the pickup into a parking lot and came to a whiplash stop. She avoided eye contact and allowed the sign above the door to capture her interest. B & B Hardware? Dani peered to her right where two lanes of gas pumps stood, and a smile wiggled onto her face. A hardware-store-slash-gas-station. Only in a small town.

She plucked a hundred-dollar bill from her purse and offered it to him. "I appreciate—"

"Keep it." Steve spat out the words and leaned away, his mouth a taut slash.

Surely he needed the money. His ragged jeans and this rattletrap he drove suggested as much. She squeezed her eyebrows together. For whatever reason, he wasn't about to take the money, so she stuffed the bill back in her wallet, shrugged off the coat, and handed it to him.

"Thanks for the ride." With a release of the door she lowered herself to the ground.

Without looking her direction, the cowboy put the truck in reverse, barely allowing her time to shut the door. As he tore out of the parking lot, his rear wheels spewed gravel.

Dani sucked in air and blew it out in a gush. Thank goodness that was over. Now to call Aunt Beth and end this nightmare. She faced the store, her heart pounding like a child on the first day of school.

Find TEXAS ROADS on Amazon in print and eBook formats.

About Cathy

A native Texas gal, Cathy currently resides in the small Texas town where she grew up. When she's not writing you'll find her digging in the dirt, rummaging through thrift stores, or up to her elbows in yet another home improvement project. In addition to the Miller's Creek novels, Cathy has also written novellas, Bible studies and devotional books. Cathy also loves to connect with readers in the following places:

| Facebook | Pinterest | Goodreads | Twitter |

To stay updated on Cathy's new book releases, visit her website at https://CathyBryantBooks.wordpress.com.

Cathy's Books

https://CathyBryantBooks.wordpress.com/books/

<u>Miller's Creek Novels</u>
Texas Roads
A Path Less Traveled
The Way of Grace
Pilgrimage of Promise
A Bridge Unbroken
Crossroads
Still I Will Follow

<u>Other Fiction</u>
Pieces On Earth (Christmas novella)
Evergreen (Christmas novella)

<u>LifeSword Bible Studies & Daily Devotionals</u>
The Fragrance of Crushed Violets
Believe & Know
New Beginnings
The Power of Godly Influence
Life Lessons From My Garden

www.ingramcontent.com/pod-product-compliance
Lightning Source LLC
Chambersburg PA
CBHW031722170626
46808CB00005B/1856